Nursery's
Rhyme

First paperback edition May 2021

Book cover design by Nihkri@fiverr

ISBN 978-1-7367-5590-7 (paperback)
ISBN 978-1-7367-5591-4 (ebook)

www.trisharrowsmithauthor.com

For my parents.

My mom, for always believing in me and supporting every dream I've had.

My dad, for his unwavering support in everything I've taken on, while simultaneously preparing me for realistic outcomes.

I love you both more than you'll ever know!

Chapter I

The rocking chair groaned as it swayed back and forth. The baby's cheek rested gently against her shoulder. She ran her hand down the front of the vintage book of nursery rhymes, her heart filled with love and longing. Her mind faded back to her own youth, to the memories of her mother reciting the same rhymes, from this exact book, night after night. She knew most of them by heart by the time she was four and could still hear her mother's voice every time she read one. Twenty-nine years later, she hoped to pass on the same tradition to her own daughter, to share the same joy she heard in those words.

She pulled herself from her tiered memories. Once again, she felt the coldness of the gravestone burrowing beneath the skin on her cheek, the book of rhymes clutched tightly to her chest. Instinctively, she wiped under her eye but the tears had dried up years ago. Opening the cover of her book, she took care to hold the pages in place. Years of use had worn the stitching holding the pieces together. She gripped the pages tighter as a breeze fluttered through the air. It was July but the weather was crisp and a light fog had navigated its way across the cemetery, hovering mere inches above the ground. She felt it closing in around her, wrapping itself around her body, tightening against her heart.

"I'm going away for a while. But I want you to know I love you, with every bit of my heart. No matter where I am, I'll always be thinking of you." She flipped to the first page and choked out the words as she stroked the side of the gravestone.

"The three little kittens, they lost their mittens, and they began to cry. Oh, mother dear, we sadly fear..."

The bass pulsated off the stage and Rock drained his glass of rum. He had milked it for nearly two hours, not feeling the desire to drink but instead the need to decompress. Francesca stopped in front of him and ran her hand over the top of his knee.

"Hey there, Rock. Want a dance?" Her lips glistened in the overhead lights and she had learned to use that to her advantage.

He remained perfectly still except for his eyes gliding up her body. "You know I don't pay for personal dances."

"One of these days, Rock. I'm gonna convince you otherwise." She winked and blew him a kiss before strutting away.

Rock licked his lips as he watched her disappear around the stage. He'd been taken by the flawless appearance of her ochre colored skin from the first time he saw her. For the last five years, she had been one of his favorite dancers. Francesca was classy, confident, and personable. The latter, not because she was trying to make money, but because, to her, it was a natural, genuine quality.

He was tempted to call her back, as he always was, when he felt the familiar buzz of his work phone in his pocket. He plugged one ear and hit the talk button with the other hand. "Rockefeller." He listened to his captain, Stone, talk as he made his way out of the bar. "I'll be there in ten." He sighed and ended the call.

Thankful for only having one drink, he slipped behind the wheel of his car and pulled onto the street.

Dixie pulled up in front of the apartment complex at the same time as Rock. With one look, it was obvious to him that she hadn't slept yet either. Her boot heels clacked on the pavement as she made her way over to his car. "Hey, Lawrence. You made it here quick." She stepped to the side to allow him room to open his car door.

"Why do you insist on calling me "Lawrence"? You know I hate it." He purposely ignored her comment about how close by he must have been. Closing his door, he towered over her and had to resist the urge to bend at the knees to look her in the eye. Rock already knew she could be a bit defensive about her petite stature even though they had only known each other for a week. Dixie transferred from a station in Georgia and hadn't yet proven herself worthy of his trust but he did give her credit for her confident attitude. She also had a fiery personality and he admired that quality in her.

"Sorry, Larry." He scowled at her and she grinned back with satisfaction. "So, what did you get for info? Crazy mother, missing infant?" They both ducked under the police tape blocking the front entrance. The tape was a pointless act assuming the abductor and infant were long gone. The idea of finding any evidence in the hallways or on any of the doors was hopeful optimism, if slightly ridiculous, in an apartment building where hundreds of residents and guests entered and exited every day.

"I'm just floored by your level of empathy. Yes, the mother seems to be inconsolable. Which, by the way, is a perfectly natural reaction to waking up and finding your infant missing from their crib in the middle of the night."

"Hey. I warned you on the first day we met that I wasn't of the empathetic variety. Besides, it makes it much easier to do a job like this. It's hard to get personally involved in a case if you're not emotionally invested in it."

"True. But that doesn't make it any less concerning."

The staircase they were climbing was stuffy and narrow. The carpet, now threadbare and faded to the hues of cement and cardboard, was once a lush, brilliantly patterned maroon and gold mix. The walls were painted a sickly, drab yellow. The heavy, metal door protested loudly when Rock opened it to allow Dixie through. The hallway was free of chatter but the pipes cried out in desperate need of repair.

They showed their badges to the officer stationed at the apartment door and stepped inside. They were pleasantly surprised by how well the apartment was maintained compared to the building. It was much larger than one would expect of any city rental. The far walls were exposed brick and the others had been recently painted. The kitchen cabinets showed little sign of wear. The same went for the carpeting and flooring.

Seeing a uniformed officer seated at the table with who they assumed was the mother, Rock and Dixie made their way to the nursery. For being a crime scene, it was aesthetically soothing. The brick wall fell behind the crib and a gray throw rug and gold ottoman were highlighted by the white furniture surrounding them. Dixie walked over to the window nestled in the corner to examine the lock. Finding it intact, she scanned the rest of the window, her eyes coming to a stop on the curtain rod. "Hey, Rock? Does this look a little out of place to you, too?" She pointed up to the makeshift clothesline hanging from the rod. Three mismatched mittens were neatly clipped to a nylon rope.

"Hm. Certainly doesn't fit with the rest of the décor. We'll ask. Maybe it's something personal to the mother? Good luck charm or something." He watched Dixie's face light up when he validated her thoughts. He rolled his eyes and turned away to survey the rest of the room.

Dixie continued her rounds of the nursery while Rock went over to speak to the uniformed officer. As far as she could tell, there wasn't anything out of the ordinary except the strung up mittens. The window was locked from the inside, all the drawers were closed, the room was tidy. If it wasn't for the empty crib, no one would guess a crime had taken place. She heard Rock whistle and he jerked his head toward the door when she looked over at him.

They walked to the kitchen to get a statement from the mother. "Chrissy? I'm Detective Rockefeller. This is my partner, Detective Lane. Is it okay if we sit down and ask you a few questions?"

Chrissy answered with a barely perceptible nod.

The uniformed officer stood and nodded at the detectives before walking away.

They both claimed a chair and watched in silence for a few moments. If it wasn't for the tears streaming down Chrissy's face, they would have thought she was in shock. Her body was slumped over and still. Behind the tears her eyes were empty. She stared into the distance, looking at nothing.

"Chrissy? Would you be able to walk us through your evening? Start with what you did right before you put Charlotte in her crib." Dixie's voice was soft and friendly.

At the sound of Charlotte's name, familiarity finally registered in her eyes. "I'm sorry. I just..."

"That's okay. Take your time. Walk us through what you did once you put Charlotte to bed."

"I really didn't do anything. I laid her down, I changed my clothes, and I went to sleep."

Dixie had taken note of her clothing when they first arrived. Fleece pajama pants and a t-shirt. "Okay. Do you keep your door locked while you're home?"

"The door automatically locks when it closes."

"Is there a father in the picture? Husband, boyfriend, anyone?"

She looked defeated by the last question. "No. Her father left the minute I told him I thought I might be pregnant. He didn't even stick around long enough to find out for sure. And, before you ask, he signed over his rights." She rubbed her eyes with the heel of her hands like a young child would do. "I called him the day I gave birth to her. That was four months ago and it's the last time I spoke to him."

"When we were in the nursery, we noticed that every item was neatly kept and it all appears to be brand new except one thing. Do the pinned mittens hold some sort of significance?"

Chrissy cocked her head to the side. "The what?"

They all made their way to the nursery. Dixie wanted to gauge Chrissy's reaction when she saw them.

"I've never seen those before." She backed up and fell to the ottoman. "Those aren't mine. Where did they come from?" Tears sprang to her eyes again and she buried her face in her hands. "Where is my baby?"

Dixie and Rock met back at the station. They agreed there was no point in either of them going home. They sat at their desks, sipping coffee, and filling out reports until Stone arrived.

Rock had never been a fan of people with more authority than he had. He had even less respect for those who believed once they reached a certain level, they didn't have to perform certain tasks anymore. Stone was one of those people. Anything short of a press conference or a fancy dinner, the only thing you could count on Stone for was to not be there. Rock despised him for that.

When he walked into the station, he came in with one coffee in hand, for himself. He went straight to his office, closed the door behind him, and booted up his computer. He had greeted them with little more than a sideways glance.

Dixie, who had only been there for a week, could feel her blood begin to boil. Her old captain, from Georgia, never would have left them alone on a case. It wasn't because he didn't trust his detectives. It was because he believed he couldn't do his job properly if he was only getting secondhand information. He needed to know what was going on. Stone was the complete opposite and Dixie was already fed up with his casual attitude. She was standing at her desk, glaring at him through the window in his office until he ripped his door open.

"Rockefeller. Now." His voice bellowed through the station.

Dixie jumped.

Rock rolled his eyes and slumped his shoulders. Reluctantly, he got up and followed Stone as he retreated back into his office. At Stone's insistence, he closed the door behind him. The two stood with arms crossed, staring at each other before either of them spoke. "How's Ella?"

Rock took a step back at the mention of his daughter. "Ella is doing just fine."

"Glad to hear it. Any more communication from the person that's supposedly been watching you?" Stone looked as uncomfortable asking the question as Rock did hearing it.

"Ahh. Thank you for your concern, but no. Nothing since the last one I told you about." He hesitated just for a moment before continuing. "Listen, Captain. I appreciate this but what's with the heart to heart? What do you really want to know?"

"Are you up to the task of leading this case? It's an infant abduction and you have a two month old at home. I need to know that you can handle this."

They locked eyes and Rock growled deep within his throat. "I resent the fact that you feel I can't keep my personal life separate from work. You do realize that I'm also married and I lead cases on missing wives all the time with no problem?"

"This is different."

"It's not different at all." Rock's jaw was clenched and he was speaking through his teeth. "I'm a missing persons' detective. People disappear, I investigate the case. It doesn't matter who it is that goes missing. This is my case and it's staying *my case*. If we're done here..." He turned and flung the door open so it bounced off the wall. He grabbed his jacket from the back of his chair and his keys from his desk drawer. "Let's go," he barked at Dixie.

Without replying, she snatched her cell phone off her desk and followed him outside.

They walked half a block before Dixie couldn't contain herself anymore. "Are you going to share what that was all about?" She could hear Rock grumbling low in his throat. She made a mental note to wear shoes with smaller heels for work as she practically had to run to keep up with his long strides.

"Just Stone being his typical self-aggrandizing...self. He thinks because I have a baby at home I'm now incapable of heading up any cases involving children." He stopped abruptly and turned to look at Dixie. "My guess? He's been doing this a long time. He probably had issues dealing with cases like this when his children were young so now he's looking for other people to have problems, too. You know, a reason for him to feel not so alone." He resumed walking but had slowed his pace considerably. When they arrived at the coffee shop, he held the door open for Dixie and ordered a large cup of coffee for both of them. "It's much better than what we get at the station." He handed her her cup and dug his phone out of his pocket. "Rockefeller."

Dixie took the time to take in the atmosphere of the shop while he was on his phone. It was much smaller than it appeared from outside. It was long and narrow. A counter ran the length of one side and four, two person tables rested against the other. The music playing was some sort of rock instrumental and was just quiet enough to get drowned out by the buzz of the machines running behind the counter.

Rock ended his call and pocketed his phone. "Looks like we're going to the lab."

He was hesitant about introducing Dixie to their forensic analyst, Gemini. The two had become close over the years they had worked together. Gemini was highly respected in her field and without her help and expertise, Rock wasn't sure he would have been able to solve any of his cases. Gemini was confident in her abilities. She was head-strong and outspoken. Rock recognized these same qualities in Dixie and knew introducing the two of them could either create a fantastic working environment or result in complete disaster.

They entered the lab and showed their badges at the front desk. Dixie couldn't help but spin around and take in the size of the building. Rock noticed and shook his head while they were waiting at the door to be buzzed in. "I told you. Gemini is good at what she does. They get a lot of funding because of her being here."

When the door opened, Dixie couldn't believe her eyes. Gemini's appearance rendered her speechless. Standing at five feet, ten inches, her skin was a rich russet and a light spattering of freckles graced her cheeks and bridge of her nose. Her eyes were solid gold that radiated from the backdrop of jet black hair that shimmered from the fluorescent lighting above.

"Dixie? Are you going to say "hi" or just stare at her awkwardly all day?"

"I am so sorry. I didn't... I just... you're... stunning!" Dixie could feel her cheeks getting hot and she knew they were glowing pink. "Forgive me. I'm not sure what I was expecting but it wasn't...you. I'm Dixie." A nervous grin crossed her face and she reached out her hand to meet Gemini's.

"You're forgiven," she replied with amusement. "I'm well aware that my appearance is a bit unusual. Rock probably should have mentioned that to you at some point." She cocked her head and gave him the evil eye.

"Probably. That certainly would have saved me some embarrassment."

"Eh. No need to feel embarrassed. I'm used to it. You should have seen Rock the first time we met. I thought I was going to have to scrape his jaw off the floor." Gemini gave her a genuine smile. "Anyway, the reason I called is because after you both left the scene last night, my crew went in to collect the evidence. It goes without saying, of course, that we took every precaution when taking down the mitten rope. Which, by the way, is one of the oddest things I've ever seen. But, the main thing is, we also found something that you guys missed in your walk-through." She reached over to the counter and handed them an evidence bag. "It's a bingo ball. Not surprised it was missed because we found it nestled up against one of the crib legs. The mother swears she's never seen it before. We took plenty of pictures for you, they're on the table by the door. I'm going to get busy processing what we have but I've gotta be honest with you. We don't have much."

"Are you kidding," Rock asked. "We have rope. We have not one, but three mittens and we have a random bingo ball. We're going to blow this case wide open."

"I adore you, Rock. Even when you make comments like that." Gemini leaned in and placed a kiss on his cheek. "I'll call you right away if we get anything."

Dixie grabbed the envelope of pictures off the counter as they walked out. "Wow. You could have warned me."

"Do you think a warning would have helped? Really?"

"Probably not. It should be illegal to look like that."

Back at the station, Dixie knocked on the captain's open door and held up the envelope. "We have pictures."

Rock pulled a rolling white board into the main room and began placing pictures to recreate the nursery. When he was done, without acknowledging Stone's presence, he began to walk through what they knew. "So far, we only have two pieces of evidence. The bingo ball under the crib here and the mittens that were hung from the curtain rod." He pointed each out as he spoke. "Both are at the lab now. There are only two ways to get in to the nursery. The bedroom door and this window. The window was locked which means the kidnapper had to come through the apartment somehow. The windows in the rest of the apartment were also locked which means?" He pointed at Dixie for her to step in.

"Which means, they must have come in through the door. Or maybe an air vent?" She paused to think for a moment. "Or...maybe Chrissy let them in even if it was unknowingly. It could be a friend or an old boyfriend with a spare key."

"Bingo," Rock said and did his best to stifle a laugh. "It's an old building so they don't have air vents like we're used to. They have radiators instead. I was thinking the same thing though. Chrissy did say she's single but we need to backtrack and find out if she has someone watch Charlotte while she's at work. We also need to see if she changed the locks after the father bailed on her."

"But she said he signed over his rights."

"Well, we do have his name. We'll double check with the courts to be sure and we'll pay him a visit just for kicks. At this point, we have nothing else to go on."

"Sounds good to me."

Rock pointed at Stone. "Captain, appreciate your input as always." He grinned and headed toward the door with Dixie on his heels.

"Remind me again why he gets paid more than us?"

Rock held the door open for her. "The bigger the asshole, the bigger the paycheck."

"Damn. He makes a lot more than us."

The two swung by Chrissy's apartment to check up on her and ask a few follow up questions. Emotionally, she wasn't faring any better than she had been when they first met. While they were there, they met her mother who, coincidentally, was also Charlotte's babysitter. They got the last known address of the baby's father and his place of employment. They asked if she had tried to contact him since Charlotte disappeared. Chrissy informed them that she had, only to find out he had blocked her number. The visit was quick but they had gained a lot of necessary information.

Assuming Richard wouldn't be home, Rock decided to stop by his house anyway. It was a short detour on the way to his job. When no one answered, he took the liberty of peeking through all the windows, looking for any sign of a child. He found nothing except the reassurance that Chrissy was correct about him still living with his mother.

Richard worked at a recycling plant on the city line. As soon as they pulled in to the parking lot their noses filled with the stench of rotting trash. There was nothing they could do to escape it. Neither of them had changed their clothes since the day before and now this smell would be embedded in the fabric.

"We may have to burn our clothes when we leave here." Dixie was talking through a hand that was covering her mouth and nose.

"I agree. And you look like a child covering your face like that."

"Oh, I know. It doesn't actually help. It's more of a barrier in case I throw up. This is a recycling plant, why on earth does it smell like rotting fish wrapped in a baby's diaper?"

"If you throw up, you're walking home. This is your only warning. And how did you ever survive in homicide if you can't handle this?"

"It was different. At least then I knew what it was I was breathing in. This could be anything."

Entering the building, the first person they found was Richard's boss. "I'll get him for you but whatever it is that you think he did, you're wrong. Richard is one of the best guys I know."

"If you consider leaving a pregnant woman to be a single mother and signing over your parental rights a stand up quality, he may be one of the best."

He had started towards the back of the plant but stopped half-way through the door. "Now, hold on a minute, Detective. That may not be morally correct but last I knew it wasn't against the law."

"It's not. Can you go get him, please?"

As soon as he walked through the door Dixie turned on Rock. "What the hell was that for?"

"Because I hate that response. We could be hunting down a mass murderer and he'd be the best guy everyone knows."

Richard came through the door and greeted the detectives. "What can I do for you?"

"We need to ask you a few questions about Chrissy and Charlotte." Dixie decided to do the talking since Rock seemed to have his mind made up about Richard.

"Who?"

Dixie stood up a little straighter. "Are you kidding me? Chrissy and Charlotte. Your ex-girlfriend and your daughter." Now Dixie had the same feeling about him as Rock did.

"She is not my daughter and Chrissy is insane." All the pleasantness in his voice had dissipated.

"Legally, she's not your daughter anymore but genetically she is. She also happens to be missing."

Richard laughed with no intention of trying to control it. "I told you she was crazy. How do you lose a baby?"

Dixie rolled her eyes and put her hand on Rock's arm to stop him from stepping in. "I know you can't be that stupid. She didn't lose her baby. Charlotte was kidnapped last night. Now, would you mind telling us why you think Chrissy is crazy?"

"Whoa, wait a minute. Why are you asking me questions? You don't think I had anything to do with it, do you? I don't talk to Chrissy. And I never even met her kid." His eyes were wide and he proved to Dixie with his questions that he wasn't as dumb as he was pretending to be.

"Whether you want to believe it or not, Charlotte is your daughter. Signing over your rights doesn't change her DNA. I'm going to ask you again, why do you think Chrissy is crazy?"

Richard shook his head. "Because, this is the third time she tried to tell me she was pregnant. I kept trying to break up with her and every time she came up with this excuse for why I couldn't. I didn't want to be with her. I finally got up the courage to leave for good and it just happened to be the time that she really was pregnant. I don't even know for sure that the kid is mine. The whole time she was pregnant she was calling my phone, calling my mom's house, calling for me here. I had to get a restraining order against her to get her to leave me alone."

"Okay. She said she called you the day Charlotte was born."

"She did. I answered the call because she called from the hospital and I didn't recognize the number. I told her not to call me again. I blocked her cell phone and the number she called me from that day. Honestly, I'm just trying to move on with my life without her constantly being in it, okay."

Dixie could see the stress and defeat taking over his body. "Have you ever seen Charlotte, even out of sheer curiosity? Did you go to the nursery when she was born or maybe try to see her when Chrissy took her to the park or out to run errands?"

"No. I swear. I want nothing to do with either one of them. I told Chrissy that from the beginning."

"You still have a key to her apartment?

Richard sighed heavily. "I left it on the table when I moved out."

"Where were you last night?"

"Sleeping." He rolled his eyes toward the ceiling. "I have to be here at six every day. I get up early. I'm usually sleeping by nine."

"Let's step back for just a moment and talk about this restraining order, which, we will be checking, by the way. The city doesn't view phone calls as a threat or as harassment. So how did you get an order against Chrissy?"

Rock was fidgeting with the car keys. He was beginning to get restless.

"I know. I looked into it when it was just the phone calls but there was nothing I could do. I got the restraining order after she showed up here, four times, demanding to speak to me. I left work one day to find her sitting on the hood of my car. I told her if her behavior didn't stop I would call the police. The next day, she showed up at my mom's house at two in the morning. She was screaming and banging on the door. Woke up the whole neighborhood. One of our neighbors called the cops and that's when I filed the order. She's nuts!"

"Was she asking for anything specific when she called or showed up or do you think she just wanted the attention or validation of some sort?"

"I think it was just attention. That was the main reason I was breaking up with her to begin with. I didn't have any room to breathe. That's also why I signed over my rights. I'm not one to shirk responsibility but I can't have her ruining my life. This may not be a luxurious job but I make a decent living. I get good hours, the benefits are amazing. I almost got fired because of the scenes she caused while she was here."

"Thank you, Richard, for your time. If we do have any other questions, we will be back."

He rolled his eyes. "Can't wait." He started to walk away but stopped to look over his shoulder. "For what it's worth, I hope the kid is okay."

Rock was on his phone before they were even back in the parking lot. He wanted verification that the restraining order was real. From the sound of his voice, it was obvious he was livid with Chrissy for not telling them about it. He put his phone in his pocket. "They're emailing a copy of the order over now." His words came out as little more than a growl. "Let's go pay Chrissy a visit, *again*."

Rock pounded on the door without letting up until he heard Chrissy's mother yelling for him to stop. When she opened the door, he didn't wait for an invitation. He barged through and leaned over Chrissy who was still sitting in the same chair at the kitchen table. "Forget to tell us something, Chrissy?"

He was so close she could feel the heat of his breath on her face. She just stared at him, her eyes and mouth open wide.

"You do realize we're trying to find your daughter, right? You're missing *four month old infant*. Every single piece of information you give us right now is important. You knew we were going over to talk to Richard and you didn't once find it necessary to tell us that he filed a restraining order against you?" He slammed the paperwork they had printed in the car against the tabletop.

"The what?" Chrissy's mother, Judy, was shocked.

"You heard him correctly," Dixie replied. "Richard had to file a restraining order against her because she was stalking him at work and disturbing the peace at two a.m. when she showed up screaming and banging on his door."

"What the hell, Chrissy?"

Tears started streaming down her face but Dixie wasn't going to let her cry her way out of it. "Uh, uh. You don't get to do that again." She pulled out a chair and sat at the table across from Chrissy. "Your daughter is out there somewhere with no way to protect herself. She could be hurt. At this point, we can only hope that she's not dead. So you're going to dry your face and you're going to sit here and tell us everything we need to know that can help us find her. We can't afford to waste any more time."

That was the first time Rock had seen Dixie angry. He was impressed and a little intimidated by her sudden change in body language and attitude. The next hour was spend with Chrissy fumbling through information about her side of the story with Richard. She generated a list of people she had had contact with throughout the past year. The list wasn't very long. Most of it would prove useless but at least now they had sufficient information.

When they got back to the car Rock sat in the driver's seat staring at Dixie. "Alright. Your turn. Your mood changed awfully quick back there. Where'd that change come from?"

Dixie side-eyed him. "I just have a problem with women who try to use tears for sympathy. Do they honestly believe if they cry all their problems will magically melt away? People will fall at their feet because they shed a tear?"

"So, you're not a crier then?"

"Ha! Not even close." She pulled the sun visor down to expose the mirror and rubbed away the eyeliner that had migrated beneath her lower lashes.

"Well, I have to admit, I'm impressed. I didn't think you had it in you. You were like a totally different person."

"I may be little, but I'm the last person someone wants to piss off."

"Noted."

"So, back to you. Why the sudden change in attitude when Richard mentioned the restraining order?"

He started the car and pulled out of the parking space. "I don't really want to talk about it."

"I'm your partner. You've made it clear that I need to earn your trust. Maybe this is a good way to do it."

He pursed his lips but gave in. "Fine. Ever since my wife got pregnant, I've had someone leaving notes and stuff on my car saying they're watching me. I don't know if it's true or if it's just someone's idea of a joke but I don't like it. Pregnant wife, fine. Newborn at home, not fine anymore."

"Oh, wow. Do you think it's a woman?"

"It's hard to say. The fact that the notes are left for me says yes. But I feel more like they're watching my wife which makes me think it's a man."

"Does Stone know?" She was hesitant to ask the question knowing how they feel about each other.

"Yeah. Against my better judgment I told him. If it gets more serious than a harmless note, he needs to have the background."

"Glad to hear that. If you need anything..."

Rock just nodded.

They finished filing their paperwork and Rock sat at his desk with his head resting on his arms. It was six p.m. and the lack of sleep was just beginning to catch up with him.

"You ready to head home, Rock?" Dixie was mentally done for the day and had been tempted to leave when Stone did.

"Nah. I think I'm going to stop for a quick drink or two before I go home. You in?"

She wasn't much of a drinker but she wasn't quite ready to go back to her empty house either. "As long as you're going somewhere that serves food. I'm starving."

The bar was small and dark. Country music blasted through the speakers mounted to the wall. It was still early in the evening and only a handful of patrons were scattered about. The tables and stools looked new but gave the impression of a half-hearted attempt of renovating the otherwise rundown building. To Dixie, it screamed "local hangout". To Rock, it said "home". They found a table buried in the corner and sat down.

"I'd recommend the cowboy burger and extra rings but I don't think I've tried anything else."

"'Boy burger and rings. Got it."

Rock stared at the table and Dixie took in her surroundings until the server came to take their order. As soon as she walked away, Gemini pulled up a chair.

"Hey! Thought I might find you guys here."

Dixie smiled. "Nice to see you again. I promise, I won't stare at you."

Gemini laughed. "It's okay. I catch Rock doing it all the time." She reached over and slapped the side of his leg with the back of her hand.

"We just ordered. Did you want anything?" Rock immediately felt a sense of relief at the sight of Gemini. She always had a soothing effect on him no matter how he was feeling.

"Mmm. Just a drink. It's been a day." She looked over her shoulder and raised her arm in the air. The bartender nodded.

"I guess you two are well known here, huh?"

"You can usually find at least one of us here at the end of the day. It's usually me." Gemini outwardly seemed so composed but it was an act for the work day. After putting in all the hours she wanted nothing more than a drink, a book, and her bed. "So, I hate to be the bearer of bad news but we didn't get a thing off the mittens or the ball. We're still going through the bedding and the items from her crib but you know how that goes. How was your day? You get anything that can help me out?"

"Help you? No. Piss you off? Maybe." Rock couldn't wait to tell her the news. "Chrissy has an ex-boyfriend, the child's father. He signed over his parental rights as soon as the baby was born." He put his hand up when Gemini opened her mouth to speak. "That's not the part that'll make you mad. He signed them over with good reason."

"There is never a good reason for that."

"Ah, but this time, there might actually be. Eight months ago, he had to get a restraining order against her because she was following him.

Almost got him fired from his job because of her nonsense."

Gemini's eyes narrowed. "Please tell me you're kidding."

"Not kidding. She got arrested and sentenced to sixty hours of community service for disturbing the peace. Apparently, the judge didn't take too kindly to that sort of conduct from a pregnant woman."

"Stand-up gal, huh? You like the ex-boyfriend for it?"

"Not me," Dixie answered, shaking her head. "I wasn't sure at first but you could physically see the stress coming over him when he was talking about it. Whether it was her intention or not, she really did a number on him. And then she didn't even tell her own mother about it."

"Would you tell your mother if you got arrested?" Gemini wasn't trying to sound cruel, but she wasn't sure her mother would be her go to person if she got arrested.

"Not a chance. But I also haven't spoken to my mother is almost twenty years so that could be why."

"Oh, honey. I'm so sorry, I didn't know."

"Eh. Doesn't bother me any. It's by my choice."

Rock and Dixie ate their food while Gemini leaned back and listened to the music. When they ordered their second round of drinks, Gemini gathered the courage to ask Rock how he was doing.

"You know I hate to ask this but how are doing, Rock? I know it's only the first day but with your baby and all?"

"Oh, Christ. Not you, too." He took a long sip from his glass before continuing. "I'm fine. Despite the insistence of Stone not believing I can handle it, I'm quite capable of separating the two. I do, genuinely appreciate your concern on the matter, however."

"I know what you're capable of. Just remember you can always call if you feel overwhelmed."

He stayed silent but reached over and touched her hand just enough to let her know he was listening. Dixie watched and for the first time she saw Rock's eyes soften. Maybe he wasn't such a hard-ass all the time after all.

Rock tried to be as quiet as he could when he walked through the door. He took his shoes off and hung his keys on the hook inside the door. He knew Ella was sleeping and he didn't want to wake her but he had a strong desire to hold her just for a minute. Until she was born, he never knew he was capable of loving another person so much. In his eyes, she was perfect. At the risk of waking her by picking her up, he opted to stand by her crib to watch her sleep. He reached out and ran his hand over her head. She barely stirred. He couldn't remember the last time he had slept that well.

He'd been on the force for sixteen years. From the very first night he began to sleep with one eye open. As a patrol officer or a detective, one could never be careful enough, especially when their family was involved.

He took a hot shower to sooth his muscles and rinse off the smell of the recycling plant before slipping under the covers and wrapping himself around his wife. This was his favorite part of every day, enjoying her warmth and feeling their bodies connect in a way that wasn't purely sexual. He felt her arm move and she embraced his hand with her own. Sleep took over almost immediately.

He awoke to the smell of freshly brewed coffee and stretched before climbing out of bed and into freshly laundered pants. He smiled at Ella, who laying in her bassinet. Her eyes widened when he entered the room. Rock scooped her up and went to the kitchen in search of coffee. His wife stood at the kitchen counter. She had just finished filling a mug for him and she pushed it in his direction. Leaning in to give her a kiss he was met with resistance as she turned her face. He barely grazed her cheek. "Good morning to you, too. What'd I do now?"

She turned and stared at him, her eyes full of rage. "Nothing. You didn't do anything, that's the problem. You haven't been home in two days."

"I was working. You know it happens sometimes. You seemed happy I was home last night, why are you yelling at me now?"

"I was happy that you were home safely. I hadn't heard from you once in two days. But I'd love to know how you 'working'" she made quotes in the air with her fingers to illustrate her point, "somehow ends up with you coming home, smelling like alcohol."

"You know having a drink helps me unwind."

"Yes, I do. And it was fine before you had a child to think about. Why can't you just come home and have a drink here? I know it sounds crazy, but you would think it would be different if you got to come home and see your daughter. Look at you. You can't even walk into the kitchen in the morning without picking her up and bringing her with you. So why is it so different at night? Why can't you just come home instead of leaving me to worry about you for days at a time?"

Rock slammed his mug on the counter, startling Ella. "I don't have time for this." He kissed his daughter on the cheek and laid her back in her bassinet before heading out the door.

Chapter II

This one won't be easy. But they may be doing the baby a favor.

The second call came in almost exactly four days after the first. Another infant gone missing in the middle of the night.

Rock woke to the sound of his cell phone ringing at one-thirty. He stumbled out of bed and grabbed the first pair of pants and shirt he found. When he arrived, he saw Dixie standing outside, speaking to a uniformed officer. "I hope you weren't waiting long. This one is a little farther away than the last."

They flashed their badges while walking through the door. "Not really. But I was still awake anyway. I don't think I've slept in two days. Did you actually get some sleep?"

"Yeah, if that's what you call an hour. You get any information from security?"

Dixie laughed heartily. "Hey. We were all rookies once, you know?"

"Oh, no. Did you really get stuck with door duty?"

"Thankfully, no. I managed to make my mark in the department pretty quick."

They approached the door and could hear a commotion coming from inside the apartment. The moment they entered a woman turned to face them. "Oh, perfect. More of the squad showing up at my apartment instead of going out and looking for my daughter." She addressed Dixie and Rock directly. "Hey. I don't know if anyone told you but you're not going to find her here. She's missing. You need to be out there." She pointed toward the door as if they were all stupid.

Dixie rolled her eyes. "This is going to be a long night." Ignoring her comments, they went directly into the nursery. The room was located toward the middle of the apartment and backed to the main hallway so there were no windows. It may originally have been designed to be a study or large closet rather than a bedroom.

They both paused when they stepped into the room. It looked like some sort of interactive science exhibit that you'd find in a museum. Every item in the nursery was a different shade of pink and decorated in ruffles. A stuffed hippo wearing a tutu sat on a rocking chair in one corner. A dust ruffle wrapped around the bottom of the crib and changing table. Decorative pillows were strategically placed around the room and covered with frills of various fabrics. Dixie tried to control herself but the lack of sleep was beginning to get to her. She erupted in a fit of giggles that grew worse the more she tried to control them.

Rock looked at her with his head cocked. "You okay? This isn't really a joke."

She took a deep breath to stop herself from laughing again. "I know. I'm sorry. It's just...there are so many ruffles in here. And some of them are so big. Look at this thing!" She raised up the edge of a pillow by the seam. "She may have actually misplaced the baby in one of these."

Rock bit his lip to stop himself from laughing at her observation.

"I can see the headline already. "Local baby, swallowed whole, by sea of ruffles.""

"I don't disagree with you but I am going to recommend you get some sleep tonight."

Dixie pinched her lips together while she turned back to continue observing the room.

Rock watched her try to focus. He watched her shoulders jump and heard a quiet snorting noise escape while she tried not to laugh. He had just turned his head away when he heard her shout.

"N thirty-seven."

"Seriously, Dixie." Rock was staring at her with his mouth hanging open. "You've got to get yourself together."

"No." She pointed to the dresser. "N thirty-seven. The bingo ball."

"What was the first one again?"

"B thirteen. Do they mean anything to you?" Dixie knelt on the floor and looked under the crib in search of any additional clues.

"Not a thing. You see anything else out of the ordinary? Mittens, clothesline, anything?"

"Just the ball."

Yelling erupted from the living room and they could only assume someone else had walked through the door. They found their way out and ran into Gemini and her forensics team. Dixie walked straight up to her. "Good luck with this one. And, FYI, you should direct your team to leave no ruffle unturned."

"What?"

Dixie was already walking away, leading the mother, Brenda, over to the couch. Gemini guffawed when she saw the room and Dixie had to clear her throat to stifle her laugh.

Rock was studying the window locks while Dixie was trying to get answers from Brenda.

"Hey. You. Man detective. Think you could go look for Lily instead of staring at my windows? She's a baby, not Spider-man."

Rock's torso rose and fell slowly as he turned toward her. "Ma'am. With all due respect, we don't need your opinions to do our job. Please, just answer detective Lane's questions." He turned back toward the window hoping he could continue to keep his cool.

Dixie brushed her hand against Brenda's knee to get her to focus her attention on the questions. "Is Lily's father still in the picture?"

"Maybe."

"Maybe? Could you elaborate a little on that?"

She slowed down her speech in an attempt to get Dixie to understand what she was saying. "He might be. I have a few who still come around. I don't actually know which one is her father."

"Okay. Honesty is best." She made notes on her scratch pad, mindful of keeping them professional. "Do any of the men have keys to your apartment?"

"Mhm. I enjoy entertaining. It's easier if I don't have to rush around to be here to let them in."

"That makes sense." Just as she opened her mouth to ask the next question, her cell phone rang. She held up one finger, looking at the screen. "Hey, Rock. Take over for a minute." She tossed him her note pad and stepped outside the apartment. "Branden? It's almost three in the morning." She waited silently while he spoke. "I won't be able to see you until late tonight but I'll call you as soon as I can, okay?" She hung up and stood in the hallway a moment before entering the apartment again. "Sorry about that. It was an important call I needed to take."

Once they were back at the station Rock sat leaning back in his chair, staring at the top of Dixie's head.

Dixie was busy filling out paperwork. She shifted her eyes to look up at him. "Did you need something?"

Rock sat up and leaned forward. "What kind of important calls are you getting at three in the morning?" He threaded his fingers and rested his head on his hands as if he were waiting for a spectacular story.

"I'm not sure that's any of your business. And, if you don't mind," she waved a stack of paper in the air, "we have an entire list of men to look up in the system. Our new friend has quite the active social life."

"Makes you wonder, doesn't it? How someone like her can have so many people at her beck and call. She's not exactly nice or all that attractive in my opinion."

"People react differently to trauma and stress. Maybe it makes her mean. I do agree with you but her ability to lure men into her web isn't what we're investigating." She halved the paper stack and tossed a pile over to his desk.

He groaned but didn't move to reach it. "So, your phone call?"

"We're working. And I'm not going to tell you so drop it, okay?"

They spent the next three hours doing background checks and scanning social media pages looking for information on all thirty-seven men Brenda had listed.

Rock groaned and rubbed his forehead with his fingertips. "Thirty-seven names. I suppose we should be thankful she was so forthcoming and we didn't have to pry it out of her like we did with Chrissy. Still, I wish she was able to narrow it down a little."

They were only able to check a few names off the list as being unlikely. Brenda wasn't choosy about who she was entertaining or who she let around her daughter. Less than eight hours ago, they had zero suspects. Now, they had a full day ahead of them and that wasn't including any additional leads they had to track down.

By the time Stone waltzed into the office both Dixie and Rock were already exhausted. They had their day planned and were getting ready to head out when he approached and asked for a full, detailed briefing about the case. Rock, unwilling to waste his time giving in depth information just so Stone could sit in his office all day, offered a condensed version with enough details to appease him.

Satisfied with the information, Stone retreated to his office while Dixie and Rock gathered their things. He appeared again, leaning against his doorframe with his arms crossed over his chest. "You still sure you can handle this, Rock?"

Rock could feel his anger rising. He glared at Stone in silence before turning and walking out the door.

Dixie called her brother back as soon as she could. She knew any time he called her it was because he was in some sort of trouble. Since he was a teenager, trouble seemed to follow him wherever he went, which also meant it indirectly followed Dixie. He wouldn't tell her why he was in the city or how he got there but she agreed to meet him in the motel he was staying at. One her way, she stopped to pick up two cups of coffee. It was a small gesture but she used it as a means to get him to open up to her about what was going on.

She neared the motel door and it swung open before she had a chance to knock. He ushered her in, poking his head out and looking both ways before closing and locking it and securing the deadbolt.

Dixie set the cups down on the desk and embraced him like she hadn't seen him in years. Every time she walked away from him, she knew it was a real possibility it could be the last time she saw him. He didn't have many friends to count on but he had plenty of enemies that were always keeping an eye on him.

"What are you doing here?" Dixie tried to keep her voice light, fighting the urge to scream at him.

"I needed a vacation." He shrugged his shoulders and flashed her an innocent smile.

Dixie slapped his shoulder. "You're full of shit. How much trouble are you in?"

"Look at you playing detective. You always were good at that game." He grabbed his coffee off the desk and sat on the side of the bed. "I'm not really in trouble. No more than usual, anyway. I just wanted to get away for a while so I thought I'd come visit. How are you?" He patted the bed next to him inviting her to sit down.

Dixie took in his appearance and felt a rush of dread come over her. He was visibly worn out. His clothes needed washing, his hair cutting, and he needed to get a good, uninterrupted night's sleep. "Honestly, I'd be better if you weren't here. I just got my first big case here a few days ago and now I'm just going to be worrying about you."

"I told you, I'm fine."

"I know better than that. Whenever you seek me out it's because you're in trouble." She swatted his knee to show him she wasn't upset. "I am glad you're here though. It's nice to see a familiar face."

"I'm happy to see you, too. I still can't believe you moved so far away."

"What's that matter to you? You've never stayed in one place long enough for it to matter where I am."

"When you were in Georgia it felt like I was going home when I went to visit you. Now that you moved, I don't have a place to go home to anymore."

They talked for almost an hour before Branden admitted that he needed money. Dixie had come prepared for the request because debt was his biggest enemy. She handed him four hundred dollars, hoping it was enough, and then an additional sixty for food and travel.

Dixie left her brother's motel room and sat in her car with her eyes closed for almost ten minutes before pulling out her cell phone. She scrolled through her contact list and hit the call button. Silently, she chanted "please pick up, please pick up," until she heard the phone click on the other end. "Hey! It's me. You interested in stopping by?"

"Give me an hour. Leave the door unlocked."

She ended the call and drove straight home. She left the lock disengaged as instructed.

He entered her house and locked the door behind him. Dixie was kneeling on the floor at the foot of her bed with her hands clasped behind the small of her back. She'd opted for the knee-high, four inch stiletto boots that he always enjoyed along with her recently purchased, corset style, leather bodysuit.

"Already on your knees. Just the way I like you." He gently ran one finger down the side of her face before cupping her chin in his hand, forcing her to look up at him. "Are you going to behave for me tonight?"

"Yes, Sir."

"Mmm. You know that's not what I want to hear." He unbuttoned his pants and pulled a pair of handcuffs from his back pocket.

The next morning Dixie walked into the station to find Rock already sitting at his desk.

He looked up at her when she entered and gave her a once over. "Wow! You look like shit."

"Well, good morning to you, too. I didn't sleep very well last night." The truth was she hadn't slept. She had a guest who needed entertaining and they both left her house at the same time.

"It doesn't look like you slept at all."

Dixie rolled her eyes and laid her head on her desk. "Wake me up before the boss gets here."

"No can do. We need to work through the rest of these names. We didn't find a thing yesterday and I have no doubt the rest of these men will be just as sleazy and just as unhelpful as the ones from yesterday. But, what do you say we head out before Stone comes in?"

"That works for me. Let's just go now, I need some caffeine anyway."

The first stop on their list was the residence of one Michael Smith. He had a record on file but it was mainly misdemeanors. He answered the door in baggy, stained jeans and a white, ribbed tank top. A half-smoked cigarette dangled from his lips and his hair hadn't been brushed, probably for days. He eyed them for a minute through half-closed lids. "Whatever it was, I didn't do it. I was home all night." He made to close the door but Rock stuck his foot in the way.

"Lucky for us, it wasn't last night. We have a few questions for you about your friend, Brenda."

He looked up at the ceiling, trying to recall the name. "Ah. Brenda. Saw her just a couple days ago. If she's dead, it wasn't me." He tried again to close the door.

Rock hit it with the side of his fist and it swung back, narrowly missing Michael's face. "Now, what would make you say something like that?" He stepped over the threshold, reminding Michael which one of them was in charge.

"I'm just sayin', it's the only reason I could think for you to be over here. Brenda's a good girl and a sure thing, that's why I go visit." He winked at Rock as if that statement somehow bonded the two men. "But I know I'm not the only one she keeps around and she's not exactly nice. Wouldn't surprise me a bit if she pissed off the wrong person."

"You have a key to her apartment?"

"I do."

"You ever use it when she doesn't know you're going over? Ever try to surprise her or go over when she's not there?"

"Nah. Brenda's just someone I call when I need to get laid and have no one else to call. We don't have, like, a relationship or nuthin.'"

Dixie stepped in behind Rock who had now fully entered Michael's house. "So, you don't care that you could be the father of her baby?"

Michael's eyes widened in shock. "Hold up. She didn't say nuthin' about me bein' that baby's daddy."

"You two always use protection?"

"That's getting a little personal, but if you must know, I prefer goin' raw."

"So it never occurred to you that it was possible for you to be the father?" Dixie was getting impatient with his incompetence.

"Not until just now."

"Did you take her?"

"Take who?"

"Lily, Brenda's little girl."

"If she's missing, I didn't do it. I don't want nuthin' to do with any kids. I told you, we don't have a relationship. I call her when I call her."

"Well, we'll call you if we have any more questions." Both detectives turned and left Michael standing in his doorway dumbfounded.

"Wasn't me," they heard him yell as they were getting in the car.

The other three men weren't forthcoming with information but Michael was the worst of the day. Rock and Dixie ended the interviews with no more information than they started with. All the men from both days admitted to seeing Brenda on occasion but none of them wanted to claim a relationship status beyond a quick hookup.

They went back to the station and had barely entered the building when Stone approached them and turned them back out the door. "We have a press conference in ten minutes."

Dixie sighed and shook her head. She was exhausted and knew she didn't look any better than she had when she got to work that morning. The last thing she wanted was to appear on television. Fortunately for her, Stone had seen some of her previous footage and wasn't ready to let her in front of the camera to represent their station. He had told her that much when she applied for the position. Dixie wasn't a fan of reporters or having a microphone shoved in her face. She had gotten into her fair share of arguments on live TV. One overly intense reporter had gone a bit too far and it ended in a physical altercation which ended with Dixie, and her entire team, under the spotlight.

Surprisingly, there were very few reporters or cameras at the conference. Dixie was used to half the city showing up. It seemed they had managed to keep the case quiet enough so far, but with no leads and two missing infants, they needed to reach out and ask the public for their help. Rock and Dixie stood off to the side while Stone addressed the people. The day had warmed up nicely but neither of the two had realized how hot the sun had gotten until they were standing directly in it. They were both wearing black suit jackets and the material was absorbing all the heat. Dixie was squinting to keep the sun out of her eyes and silently hoping the cameras weren't trained on her face.

"...so we're asking you, if you have any information about these two children, please reach out to us. And, if you have a young child, especially if you are a single parent, please take the necessary precautions while you're at home and call us immediately if you notice anyone paying particular interest to your child." The reporters that were present swarmed in and started yelling their questions to be heard over the others. Stone, not so politely, declined any further comment on the matter and turned his back toward the cameras.

Leila Romero stormed into her boss's office. "I want this story," she demanded.

"And so we're on the same page?"

"The infant abduction. I got there just as they were wrapping up a conference that no one told me about." Her accusatory tone was evident but she hadn't intended to hide it.

"I didn't know about it. I was with Jack getting footage about the murder over on South Twenty-second. Why do you want this?" John was tough to work for. He was demanding and didn't work well with others. His attitude clashed with his appearance. He was barely forty but sported a large belly, thick, round glasses, and a head of rapidly thinning brown hair. He looked more like an errand boy than a high-powered boss.

"Two infants. Both abducted from their homes overnight within a week. The parents are single mothers. Missing persons has a new detective, some tiny blond girl I've never seen before and of course, Lawrence is taking lead. From what I managed to gather while I was there, they don't have any suspects yet. They're asking for public help."

"If they want it public, they can have it public. It's yours. Keep me updated."

Leila turned on her heel and headed to her desk. She was surprised he fulfilled her request so promptly. She booted up her computer and began a search for public police logs. She had a few back ways to find information the public didn't have access to but for now, she was focused on the calls themselves. She only needed to know where the abductions took place. There were hundreds of calls to dig through and no easy way to filter the results. As soon as she found the addresses the police were dispatched to, the rest would fall into place. After nearly two hours of searching she had two addresses, the mothers and infant's names and ages, and the times the abductions took place. She printed the information she found, powered down her computer, and headed out the door.

Chrissy's apartment was closest to the station so she decided to go there first. She didn't have a list of questions planned. She was going to ask as many questions as Chrissy was willing to answer. She opened the door after the first knock.

"Oh, hi. Can I help you?"

"Chrissy, right? I'm Leila Romero, reporter for The Local Sun. I'm sure you saw the press conference today. I was wondering if I might be able to come in and ask you a few questions. I promise I won't take too much of your time. I'd just like to follow up the conference with some first-hand information from you." She had stepped forward enough so Chrissy wouldn't be able to close her door. Over the years, she had learned that the less time you gave people to say "no", the more time you gave them to say "yes". Once she started talking, she didn't give people a chance to get a word in until she had them backed into a figurative corner.

"I'm sorry, I'm not really up to talking right now. Can I ask, though, how you got my address? The detectives assured me that my identity would remain confidential and I believe," she pointed directly at Leila, "you're one of the reasons why."

Leila took another step forward. "It doesn't surprise me that the detectives weren't one hundred percent truthful with you. Technically, no, your name isn't made public. But the call logs to the police are. Anyone that knows where to find the logs has access to the address the police were dispatched to. A quick internet search will give you all the rest of the information."

Chrissy had to think about it for a moment. "So, you stalked me to get my personal information?"

"Of course not. I'm a reporter, I do research for a living."

"Well, you'll have to try a little bit harder because I'm not giving you any information. Now, get out of my apartment before I call the police again."

"If you change your mind, here's my card."

"Out," Chrissy shouted without reaching for the card. She closed the door and watched Leila's business card slide under it.

Leila wasn't surprised she got turned down but she had high hopes she might hear back from Chrissy in a few days. Figuring she would fare better with Brenda, she stopped and grabbed a quick bite to eat at a cafe on her way. At Brenda's, she knocked on the door and could hear a commotion coming from inside. She had just raised her fist to knock again when the door flew open.

"What?"

"Hi." She smiled as wide as she could without it seeming fake. "I'm Leila Romero, reporter for The..."

"Nope." Brenda slammed the door in her face.

Feeling defeated, Leila drove back to the news station to plan her next move.

Chrissy dug Rock's business card from under a stack of papers on her desk. She called him almost immediately after Leila left. She refused to let him speak until she told him the entire story.

"Can I talk now?" When Chrissy didn't reply he continued. "So, I just want to make sure I have this all straight. A reporter showed up at your house and asked if she could interview you. She stepped into your apartment without being invited. And you're calling to file a report because she was stalking you? Is that correct?"

Dixie was sitting at her desk staring at him, trying to ask him who he was talking to.

"Yes! She said she used the internet to find all my information." She sounded almost hysterical.

Rock had to take a minute to stop himself from laughing. "So, you're upset because she did the exact same thing to you that you were doing to Michael?"

"Ugh. That's different. She's not carrying my child."

"You've got me there. I can log this call for you but there's nothing we can do about someone knocking on your door no matter how they found out where you live."

"But what about her being in my apartment? You must be able to do something for that."

"If you were holding the door open, there's nothing we can do. You said yourself when you asked her to leave, she did. That's not stalking and it's not harassment. People have the right to knock on your door. As far as her being a reporter, annoying as it may be, asking you for an interview is part of her job. If she comes back, call us."

"Well, thanks for nothing. I thought protecting people was your job?"

"Finding missing people is my job. But either way, based on what you've told me, she didn't do anything wrong."

"Fine."

"Chrissy. If she, or any other reporter approaches you again, do not talk to them. I can't stress that enough."

She hung up without another word.

Rock pulled up Brenda's file and called her to warn her that someone may go try to talk to her. She was not at all interested in what he had to say. He hung up the phone and turned his attention to Dixie. "Looks like we have an interested reporter. Leila Romero. Stay alert. This one doesn't play nice."

"Ooh, fun. Now I have something to look forward to."

All the available nurses hovered around the television watching the news replay the press conference. They all silently wondered if either of the missing infants was one they had helped deliver or care for. They wondered if they knew the mother. Being around newborns during the first few days of life, the nurses felt a special bond with them and were always torn when they left. They were happy to see them strong enough to go home and sad they had to say goodbye. The babies became a large part of their lives, even if it was only for a few days.

"This is heartbreaking."

"Unbelievable. And sad. What kind of person would take a baby? It's just not right."

"I can't imagine what the mothers are going through. There are some crazy people out there."

"Speaking of, I'm going to go check on the babies."

They all filtered out of the room, none of them willing to admit what was implied.

"It isn't possible for someone to walk out of the hospital, unnoticed, with a newborn, is it?"

Chapter III

She wasn't meant to be a target. She's merely a matter of convenience.

Rock woke up feeling refreshed which was rare for him. He took some time to do some cardio, he ate a banana and a bran muffin, and made coffee to bring to the station with him. He was feeling energized and focused. The previous evening he had made a concerted effort to go straight home from work and spend quality time with his wife and daughter. The evening was relaxing and free of any arguments and drama that had become an expected and typical part of their relationship.

Today he had a little spring in his step as he made his way out to his car. His good mood dissipated when he got behind the wheel and noticed the piece of paper tucked under his windshield wiper. He closed his eyes and took a deep breath before reaching in to his glove box to pull out a pair of gloves and an evidence bag. He hesitated before reaching out to grab the note.

Larry,

I'm sorry to hear about the new case you're working on. It must be awful for you having a newborn at home that's almost the same age. I really hope you're able to keep her safe.

Yours truly!

Rock took out his phone and snapped a picture of the note before dropping it in the bag. He didn't bother to seal it, just tossed it onto the seat next to him. He sent the photo over to Stone and tore out of his driveway before calling him. "Hey, it's Rock," he said before Stone had a chance to speak. "Did you get the text I just sent?"

"Opening it as we speak."

"I'm going to be a little late to the station. I'm swinging by the lab first to drop this off with Gemini."

"Oh, shit. Your stalker called you by your name."

"Mhm, for the first time. Odd that whoever it is chose 'Larry' though. Anyway, you see what else they mentioned?"

"You're going to have to fill me in here."

"The ages. We never said how old the missing babies are, we only ever referred to them as infants."

"I see that now. You think it could be a coincidence? Just generalizing and guessing at an age range?"

"It could be," he beeped at the car before him that was sitting still at a green light, "but I'm not convinced. I'll see you in a while." He hung up his phone and pulled around the car in front of him, waving his middle finger as he drove by. He wanted this note to be top priority for Gemini and didn't want to catch her in the middle of anything else.

He had to wait in the lobby area of the lab for nearly five minutes before Gemini came out drying her hands. "Hey, Rock. Come on back."

"Thanks for meeting me unexpected. I'm really hoping you're not terribly busy this morning?" His voice had a pleading tone to it.

Gemini laughed. "You know better than that. I'm always busy. What can I do for you?"

He handed over the unsealed evidence bag. "I got a new note on my car this morning."

Gemini took it from him and read it silently. "Oh. You're on a first name basis now? And you're going by Larry?" She looked confused. "When did that happen?"

"I thought that was weird, too. You know I haven't gone by Larry since my first year on the force." He could see that she was reading the note over and over. "I mean, some people think they need to earn the right to call me 'Rock' but, if this person has been watching me, you would think they would know what to call me."

Gemini held up one finger. "Unless..." she read the note one more time. "Unless it's someone you knew from back in the day. When did you say you started getting notes from this person?"

"It was just after Jill and I found out we were pregnant. The very first note said they knew about the pregnancy but we hadn't told anyone yet. Either way, I had just moved here when I became a detective so I know very few people here that would call me that. This makes me think it's someone from Jill's past. If they're watching her, they would know she calls me "Larry".

Rock had received the first note the day after they got confirmation from the doctor. Now, almost a full year later, it still didn't make any sense to him. The first note congratulated them on the pregnancy and then asked if they were going to keep this one. Rock assumed that first one was meant for his wife but he didn't tell her about it. They respected each other's privacy and that included past relationships. He also didn't want to stress her out or make her think that someone was watching or following her. Every month after that, he received another message from the stalker letting him know that they were watching him. None of the messages contained any personal information. Taking out the fact that they were left on his car, they could have been meant for any pregnant woman in the city. That was the main reason Rock was so concerned about this latest one. Why are they getting personal now? Is it actually personal? Are they just now getting the information? Is it because of the case he's currently working? At this point, he didn't have any idea and he wasn't sure he wanted to.

"Okay. I'll see what I can get off this. You'll need to give me a few hours, though. I don't have the manpower to work on it right this minute."

"As soon as you can get anything, I'd really appreciate it. I don't like it feeling this personal."

"I understand. You, um...you told Stone, yes?"

Rock nodded just once. "Of course. But I didn't have a choice. I had to let him know I was going to be late." He grinned at her and leaned in to kiss her on the cheek. "Thank you." He left hoping he would hear back from her soon. One of these times, this person has to leave some sort of evidence behind.

Dixie greeted him when he walked in to the station. "I was worried I might be working by myself today."

Rock sat at his desk. "Sorry. I just had something I had to take care of before I came in today."

"Rock." Stone had made his way to his office door and gestured for Rock to join him. "What'd Gemini say?"

"She'll work on it. She's busy but she'll try to get to it within a couple hours."

"Fine. Let me know if you hear back from her. In the meantime, I want you to take one of the dashboard cameras for your car. Turn it on when you head in for the night. Let's see if we can get someone on camera."

"I don't really think that's necessary, I..."

"It's not an option. Right now, even if it is merely a guess, the fact that this person knows the ages of the babies means we need to see if we can find out who it is. They may have information that can help us in the case. It's also getting more personal now with them addressing you by name. Starting tonight, you're required to have the dashboard camera on your car."

"How far up the chain of command did you go?"

"As far up as I had to, to make sure my detectives are kept safe."

Rock nodded and went back to his desk. He appreciated Stone's concern and simultaneously loathed his lack of respect for his personal life.

"All good?" Dixie knew she shouldn't pry but the drawn look on his face made her curious.

"Yeah, all good. Let's head out and see if we can catch up with Chrissy and Brenda. Someone must have contacted at least one of them by now."

"Aside from the reporter, what's her name?"

"Leila. Yeah. I'm honestly a little worried Brenda may have talked to her just to spite us." As soon as the words came out of his mouth he couldn't help but wonder if one of the women had spoken to Leila. Maybe that's how the person leaving him notes knew the ages. "Give me just a minute." He stood and went back to Stone's office. "Hey, Captain. You didn't hear about any news reports or articles about the case this morning or last night, did you? Aside from the one we authorized."

Stone shook his head.

"Leila Romero stopped by Chrissy's yesterday. She swears she didn't tell her anything but, we're going to talk to the two ladies now."

He nodded. "Keep me updated."

Rock was hesitant to tell Dixie what was going on but he knew he didn't have a choice. He didn't want her hearing about it from anyone else, which he knew was bound to happen. More importantly, he needed her help in keeping their line of questioning accurate so they could determine if either of the two women had actually spoken to Leila. He had doubts about both of them. Chrissy said she didn't talk to her but she also hadn't been honest with them right from the start. Rock had a hard time believing that she would be honest with them now. Brenda he worried would talk to a reporter just to piss them off without thinking about any further consequences of her actions. There are reasons detectives don't release all the information they have during press conferences and interviews. It's because they need to keep some information secret in order to interrogate any potential suspects. More often than not, suspects call themselves out by accidentally revealing information that only the guilty party would know. They had purposely kept the ages secret for that exact reason. They also wanted mothers to take extra precautions if they had young children but they didn't want to cause any unnecessary stress or fear. So far, only two babies had been kidnapped and that wasn't enough for them to definitively say any future victims wouldn't be of a different age. This early in the investigation, anything they find has to be considered coincidence and not fact.

Rock filled Dixie in on their way over to Brenda's apartment and she nodded in understanding. He was glad she didn't pry any further.

The visits to the two apartments proved to be fruitless. Both women swore they didn't talk to Leila and neither of them could provide any more information than they already had. They were still at Chrissy's when Rock's phone rang. Gemini. He excused himself and stepped outside.

"I hate to tell you but we got nothing. Again. Whoever is doing this is paying attention. Generic pad of paper, your everyday ballpoint pen, no fingerprints, no fibers."

Rock breathed heavily into the phone. "What about the handwriting? I know it's a long shot but can you get anything from that?"

"I already looked, in case we had something to compare it to. I started sending the others to our handwriting expert a few months ago. I scanned and sent the new one over first thing. It's definitely the same person but the only thing we have so far is that, based on the angle of the lettering and where they hesitate while writing, it looks like they're writing it with their left hand. But they are right handed."

"Well, that narrows it down to what? About ninety percent of the population?" Rock's shoulders dropped and he stood staring at the ground.

"Sorry, Rock. We're trying."

"No, I know you are. You can't find evidence that isn't there." He almost hung up and then stopped. "Hey, did Stone tell you he's requiring me to use a dashboard cam?"

"Mhm. He did. And I agree with him. I already know you want to push back and I don't blame but, Rock. It's not just you you need to look out for right now. You need to think about your wife and Ella, too."

"I know. It's just...privacy and all, you know?"

"I understand. But whether you feel it directly or not, you have someone, a random stranger for all you know, invading your privacy possibly as we speak."

"Shit."

Gemini heard the realization settle into his voice. "Like I said, think of your wife and daughter."

Rock hung up his phone and paced back and forth until he felt he was composed enough that his voice wouldn't give him away. He called his wife to tell her about the note and warned her to be careful if she went out.

Without any new leads, the day dragged by. Rock felt himself spiraling downward. He started out having a great morning and it had quickly gone downhill. He went home for three hours after work and had dinner with his wife. He played with Ella and read her a bedtime story which he rarely got to do. Once his wife had retired for the evening, Rock changed his clothes and headed out the door.

The club was busier than usual and it didn't take long to see why. It was like an all-star cast with the lineup of dancers performing. All of Rock's favorites were there. He claimed his seat and leaned back ready for a full night of entertainment. Francesca was the first to see him and winked at him from the stage. Summer, his favorite fiery blond, followed closely behind and made a point to give him a show that was a little closer up. She always let him know she appreciated his patronage even though he'd refused her advances both in and out of work. As soon as she exited the stage she walked over to him and sat on his lap.

"Hey there. How are you?"

After a brief exchange she stood and leaned forward to whisper in his ear, resting her hands on the back of his chair. "Whenever you decide you want that dance," she licked the full length of his ear from bottom to top causing him to stir in his seat, "you let me know. I'll throw in a little something extra." She ran her hand up the inside of his thigh and then walked away without looking back.

Rock growled, thankful the music was loud enough that no one could hear. He refocused on the stage and watched Vixen, Porsche, and his favorite red-head, Starlight entertain him before his phone vibrated in his pocket. "Son of a bitch," he mumbled, knowing his evening had just started. He left the club to head to another missing infant scene, exactly four days from the last.

Rock pulled up to the apartment complex and didn't see Dixie's car anywhere. He was surprised he made it before her. It was eerily quiet in the neighborhood even for being two in the morning. There were no streetlights in the area but the sky was clear and the moon was bright. Rock leaned against his car, enjoying the cool air when he heard Dixie's car. He gasped when he saw her step out. His eyes moved up her body, pausing on each piece of her outfit. She was wearing high heeled shoes, a short, tight leather skirt, and she threw a suit jacket over what appeared to be a cropped, corset top. The ensemble was radiant against her blond hair and the silver and black makeup that surrounded her eyes. Until that moment, Rock had only seen her in a professional manner.

"Shut up," she warned. "I was out. And a bit far away from home. I didn't have time to change."

"I didn't say a word." Rock grinned at her and even in the dark she could see the interested flicker in his eyes. "Ladies first," he gestured her forward with his hand.

Dixie rolled her eyes and walked toward the door. She could feel his eyes on her the entire way. "You just get here?"

"Yeah. I was out as well. I can't wait to see what kind of fresh hell we're walking into this time."

"I'm just hoping we get something from this place to go on. So far, we don't have jack shit and I don't like cases like that. Even if a lead doesn't pan out, it's still better than nothing."

"Agreed." Rock observed the building as they entered and determined it to be low-income housing. Chips of muddy, brown paint littered the carpet, doing little to cover the cement flooring below. Dark patches blossomed on the ceiling showing signs of new and old water leaks. The apartment didn't appear to be in any better shape. There was a gap between the bottom of the door and the floor, the walls had yellowed over the years, and the laminate on the kitchen floor was peeling up at the edges. The furniture was sparse and there didn't seem to be much of a personal touch added to anything.

The nursery was clean and it was obvious that Melinda had put what money she was able into making it a soothing place for her daughter. Harper's name graced the wall in carved, wooden letters behind a white, metal crib. A cream, fuzzy throw rug covered the center of the room and a toy net full of stuffed animals hung in the corner.

"Dixie, check it out." Rock pointed to the crib.

Dixie peered over the top railing. In the center of the mattress was a low cut work boot sprouting dog bones from the opening. "What the hell is that?" Her lips curled up in disgust. "I'm going to say it's a pretty safe bet this isn't what Harper has been being fed."

Rock snapped a picture with his phone. "Great minds do think alike. Let's see if we can't find a ball somewhere around here." As soon as the words came out of his mouth he heard Dixie's phone ring and she frowned when she looked at the screen. Rock could hear the voice on the other end but couldn't make out what they were saying.

She ended the call and slipped the phone back into her jacket pocket. "Good thing the night's still young. That was Brenda."

"Better you than me. What'd she want?"

"She found our missing clue."

"What is it?"

"She wouldn't say. She just said we needed to get there soon, before it disappears, whatever that means."

"Excuse me, detectives? I think this might be what you're looking for." A uniformed officer was gesturing toward the net of stuffed animals. He stepped out of the way to let Rock and Dixie see.

Nestled between a brown rabbit and yellow duck was the bingo ball. G forty-eight. "Thank you," Rock nodded his approval to the officer.

The forensics team entered without Gemini. Dixie showed them what they had found so far and left to speak to Melinda. She was near inconsolable. Tears streamed down her face and she was pulling in short breaths of air. Dixie led her to the table and pulled out one of the two mismatched chairs for her. After getting answers to the basic questions, she dug a little deeper, hoping Melinda would be forthcoming with pertinent information. "Is there a father in the picture?"

Melinda sucked in a few quick breaths. "Not really. Her dad gives me money when he can but he isn't really part of her life."

"And how do you know him?"

"Travis and I were friends. We've known each other for years. We were hanging out here, watching a movie, and I guess we were both vulnerable that night. We'd never done anything like that before. We tried to hang out a few times after that but it wasn't the same. There's a tension between us now and it doesn't feel right anymore. We decided it would be best if we didn't see each other for a while. But that was before I found out

I was pregnant." She looked down at the table and shook her head. "He's been really great about the whole thing. I mean, he could have just walked away but he tries, you know."

"Has he met Harper?"

"A couple times. He came to see me when she was born. He's stopped by a few times to give me some money. He can't really afford much. I guess you can probably tell I can't either. But he's putting in an effort. It's more than I expected him to do."

Dixie wasn't a counselor and had never tried to be. She had the skills and training necessary to pry information out of people but didn't have the patience nor desire to listen to people's problems. She changed the subject and compiled a list of names and phone numbers of everyone Melinda was close to and people who had been to her apartment since Harper was born. It was a short list but it was a relief that she was willing to give up the names so easily. Maybe Melinda would actually be able to help them catch the kidnapper.

Just before four, Rock and Dixie made it to Brenda's apartment. She was still awake and opened the door almost immediately.

"Nice of you to show up. I called almost two hours ago." She stepped to the side, rolling her eyes, so they could enter.

"We were out working a case. We got here as soon as we could." Rock wasn't in the mood for playing games with her. "You said you found something?"

"Yup. And you guys took so long it almost wasn't here for you to see." She stomped her way to the nursery and reached in to turn the light off. "Look at the ceiling."

They both looked up and saw what she meant when she said it could disappear. A large diamond, made up of what could be hundreds of small, glow in the dark stickers, was perfectly placed on the ceiling.

"How could someone have had time to do this? It must have taken them hours and I wasn't asleep that long. I haven't gotten that much sleep at one time since before Lily was even born. Do you think they were in my house when I wasn't here?" She turned the lights back on.

For the first time since they met her, Dixie and Rock saw genuine concern in her eyes. Her attitude was no match for the fear that was currently being presented. "It's possible, but unlikely. To break in once is one thing but it's too risky to come in a second time. Plus, if they came in to place the diamond first, it could have alerted you if you saw it. If they did it after they took Lily, they'd have to know there are police everywhere." He turned the lights off again. "Still, you're right. This must have taken quite a while to do." They walked back toward the entry door. "I'm going to call the forensics team and have them come back out here. I don't know how soon they'll get here." He held up a finger and went back to the nursery to take a picture with his phone. It was blurred but it would work. "I'll get them over as soon as I can."

He called Gemini as they were leaving. "I hope you weren't planning on sleeping tonight."

"Nah." Her voice was groggy. "Who needs sleep? What's up?"

"I know your team is busy at the new place but I need them to go back to Brenda's when they're done. I'm sending you a picture now. She found the clue we were missing."

Gemini adjusted her eyes and tried to focus on the text that came through. "What is that?"

"Diamond. Made up of hundreds of glow in the dark stars. Says she didn't put it up and has never seen it before."

"What the hell? I'll grab a few of my guys and meet them over there. Thanks, Rock."

He shoved his phone in his pocket and pulled out his keys. "I need coffee. Hop in my car, there's a place right down the road that opens at five."

Dixie nodded and followed him. "You go home at all tonight?"

"I know you went home long enough to change your clothes. Which, by the way, you should do again before you go to the station this morning." He gave her a once over under the light of the street lamp. "You do look great, though."

She smirked. "You're a pig. And I have clothes in my car. I always keep at least two outfits in it as backups." She stared at the side of his face.

He could feel her eyes burning into his skin. "What?"

"You didn't answer my question."

He sighed. "I did go home for a few hours. Then I went out again." Rock didn't elaborate so Dixie left it alone.

They got coffee and Rock brought Dixie back to pick up her car.

When she arrived at the station, Dixie ran in, thankful she made it before most of the other's started their shift. She changed her clothes and took the time to redo her makeup to give herself a more professional appearance. When she walked back to her desk, Rock ran his eyes up and down her body. "Hmm."

"What?"

"I think I like the other you better." He smiled wide and winked at her.

"Oh, shut it. You're the one who told me to change, you have no right to complain." She laughed and sat down to start working on her paperwork. She hated to have work left over at the end of the day. Once they came back to the station for the last time, she wanted to grab her stuff and go home, not sit at her desk for hours completing a day's worth of reports.

The two took a few minutes to plan their course for the day. The first stop would be

Travis's house. The hope was to catch him before he left for work. They sat in silence for nearly two hours before Stone came in. "Morning, Dixie. Rock," he pointed towards his office.

"And so it begins." He got up from his chair and followed him into his office. "Good morning."

"I thought I told you there was no choice in regards to the dash cam?" His face was stern and his tone matched.

"Are you watching the live feed from home?" Rock sounded disgusted and he was.

"That's not the point. I was explicit in my instruction and you blatantly disregarded what I said."

"No, you told me I needed to turn it on overnight. I went home for less than three hours yesterday and then I went out. I was still out when you called me. I haven't been home since. Unlike you, when we get a call, I actually go to it."

Stone's face reddened and his jaw tightened. "Are you done?"

Rock pursed his lips and stared at him with his head cocked to the side. His arms were crossed over his chest and he was leaning with his back against the door. "I don't need some camera invading my personal privacy. If I'm home overnight, I will turn it on. You can watch my driveway all you want. But I don't need a second person following me around. One is more than enough. Where I go, in my personal time, is none of your business." He stared at Stone for another minute waiting for him to speak before turning around and leaving without being dismissed. "Ready?" he asked Dixie and headed to the car.

Dixie powered down her computer, grabbed her jacket, and ran after him. She had barely caught up to him by the time he started the car. "What was that about?"

"That damn camera. Same as yesterday. He's pissed because he couldn't watch my driveway last night while I slept."

Dixie squinted. "You weren't home. And he's the one who called you or did he forget that while he was lying in bed sleeping?"

"That was exactly my point. I told him I wasn't home and he didn't seem to care. I guess I'm supposed to let him watch my car no matter where I go. Next time, I'm going to strap the camera to my forehead and let him follow me to a strip club. Maybe then he can be pissed off about seeing how much fun I'm having as a married man when he can't get his own wife to look at him.

Dixie laughed out loud until tears sprang to her eyes. "Oh my god! Is that really where you were?"

"Actually, it is. Kind of wish I thought to bring it with me. He could have watched one of the dancers sit on my lap...for free."

Dixie just about lost control with that last comment. "I would pay for that footage...and to see him lose his shit while he watched it."

They pulled up to Travis's house about twenty minutes after leaving the station. He wasn't far from Melinda's apartment. They got there just in time to see him stepping onto his porch. Dixie opened her door and yelled his name before he had a chance to go any farther.

"Yeah. Can I help you?" He was the most presentable so far. Donning a pair of black khakis and a grey polo, his hair was neatly combed and his shoes still held a dull shine.

Dixie hurried out of the car. "We just have a couple of questions for you. We won't keep you long. I'm Detective Lane, this is Detective Rockefeller."

Travis looked concerned for a moment. "What is it that you think I can help you with?"

"We got a call to go to Melinda's apartment last night. Your daughter, Harper, has been kidnapped."

His eyes grew wide and the color drained from his face. "Oh, god. Is Melinda okay? Did you find Harper yet?" He leaned back against the house for support.

"No, we didn't find her yet, that's why we're here. And Melinda is doing about as well as can be expected."

"You don't think I did anything, do you? I know I haven't really been around much but I try to at least help out." His breathing became more rapid and he looked terrified at the thought of being accused of taking his own daughter.

"Can you tell us where you were last night?"

"I...I was here. Home. I don't really go out often."

"Is there anyone that can verify that you were here? Did you have any company?"

"No. I was here by myself. I mostly messed around online all night."

"Your search history can verify that you were home." Dixie said it as a means to reassure him but saw the worry in his eyes. "We don't care what you were looking at. The time stamps are all we need."

Travis nodded and led them inside. His house was small. It smelled of stale food and was in desperate need of a long visit with a vacuum cleaner. Like Melinda's apartment, it was furnished with only the necessities. He swung his arm around, "it's not much, but it's mine."

While Travis was busy with the computer, Rock took it upon himself to look around the rest of the house. Finding nothing of immediate particular interest, he met them back in the living room.

Travis didn't need any additional prompting to provide a printout of his search history.

"Thank you," Dixie said as she took the papers from him. "Do you still have a key to Melinda's place?"

"I never had a key. We were only friends. We had sex once and it ruined our friendship. It's weird now."

"That happens sometimes. We'll call you if we have any other questions. Thank you for your time." Dixie turned to leave.

"Is it okay if I call Melinda? I'm really worried about her."

"Of course. I think she'd appreciate that."

About halfway back to the car, Rock stopped and looked back at the house. "Weird guy."

"He wasn't so bad. Not like the others we've met so far."

"I'm not marking him off the list just yet."

"Why? Did you find something?"

"Maybe not. There's just something I don't quite trust."

Dixie climbed into the car. "I think you're too used to people lying to you. You're starting to not trust those who are telling you the truth."

"It's not about lying. You saw his house. It looks like it hasn't been cleaned for months. It smells like rotting food and he didn't make any move to lock it when he was leaving."

"What does that have to do with anything?"

"I went into his bedroom. Everything in it was pristine. His sheets were crisp, his clothes were all folded perfectly, there wasn't a speck of dust anywhere and it smelled...clean."

"Maybe he likes to sleep in fresh sheets."

"His keeps his closet door locked. Not just with the doorknob. Three sets of locks on the door."

Dixie glanced at him from the corner of her eye. "Now that's interesting."

After stopping by the lab to pick up the latest batch of pictures, they went back to the station to piece together what they had so far. On the white board, they had a list of bingo ball numbers, a line of pictures with the additional clues they hadn't figured out yet, and two complete nurseries with possible suspects listed next to them. Rock busied himself placing pictures of the current nursery. He placed the last one and took a step back to look at what they had. He picked up a dry erase marker. "Okay, go. What do we have?"

"Method of entry is the door. The suspect has to have a key."

"Good." Rock wrote on the board: Entry: Door- Key. "What else?"

"They're all single mothers." Dixie tapped her pen on the desk she was sitting on. "But with different reasons. We have one whose father signed over rights, one who doesn't know who the father is, and one whose father helps sometimes."

"And the mothers?"

"Also different. One is a liar and a stalker, one is rude and a little too honest, at least for my liking, and the other is, possibly still in shock?" She thought for a minute. "And the relationships. One was an actual relationship gone wrong, one was nothing but sexual, and the last was a friendship ruined by a single night of passion." She couldn't help but laugh. "Geez, this is certainly making things much easier for us."

"What about the mother's ages?"

Dixie flipped through her notebook. "Twenty-six, thirty-four, and twenty-eight."

"Damn. We have nothing to go on here. Everything is different: their age, location, relationship status, personality, father figure." Rock grunted and threw the marker across the room, leaving a streak of blue running down the far wall. He inhaled deeply and slowly blew it out in an attempt to regain his composure.

"Wait a minute." Dixie hopped off the desk and picked up the marker. "We do have a couple of things that are consistent. She spoke as she wrote. "All the entries had to be the same. The mothers are all single. And," she pointed to a picture of Lily, "the babies. All three infants are female and all three are the same age. It may not be much to go on, but it's something."

Just after eight Melinda heard a knock on her door. She opened it just wide enough to see who was there. "Hi."

"Good morning. Are you Melinda?"

"Yes. What can I do for you?"

She stuck her arm through the door opening to shake Melinda's hand. "I'm Leila Romero. Reporter for The Local Sun. I'm covering the story of recent baby abductions. I'm so sorry to hear about what you're going through. I was hoping I might be able to ask you a few questions."

"Are you working with the police?" Melinda was beginning to ease the tension she had against the door.

"I cover a lot of cases the police are working on. I help to get information out to the public so the detectives can focus more on the case itself." She gave a small smile in hopes to win over Melinda's trust.

"Oh, okay. Um, you're not taking any pictures are you? I look like a mess." She patted her hair as if to show what she was talking about.

"No pictures. Just questions." She stepped through the door that Melinda had opened wider and made herself at home on the couch. Now she could see why Melinda didn't want any pictures taken. It was clear that she either hadn't slept yet or she hadn't brushed her hair since she woke up early that morning. Her tank top was stained and the bottom seam was coming unraveled. She didn't have a bra on and her fleece pants were starting to mat together from possible years of use. Her eyes were red and puffy and she still had a few streaks of mascara visible on her cheeks. "Let's start with some basic questions if that works for you. How old is your baby and what is his or her name?"

"Her name is Harper and she just turned four months old." Saying her name out loud brought fresh tears to her eyes.

"That's a beautiful name. Are you a single mom or is Harper's dad around?"

Right on cue, Melinda's phone rang and she excused herself to answer it. When she stepped into the kitchen, Leila got up and took a stroll through the nursery taking pictures on her phone as she went. She returned just in time for Melinda to come back out. "I'm so sorry. That was perfect timing. That was Harper's dad, Travis. We're not actually together but he's going to come over for a little while. I hope that's okay." She wiped the remaining tears from her cheeks and sat back down.

"That's great. I mean, I was going to ask him for an interview as well so the timing is perfect." She continued asking questions for the next fifteen minutes until Travis got there. She gave them a few minutes to themselves and when they joined her in the living room, Leila introduced herself and directed her questioning to him.

"Has Detective Rockefeller been over to see you yet?"

"Um, yeah," Travis replied. "They stopped by first thing this morning and left right before I called Melinda."

"Did they tell you why they were there?"

"Of course. I'm surprised they would think I had anything to do with it but I guess I understand. It's a usual thing, right? If a child goes missing they look at the parents, the same way they look at a spouse if something happens to their significant other?"

"Uh, huh. How many children, exactly, do they think you have? Or, if you'll allow me to back track, how many children *do* you have?"

Travis furrowed his brow and pouted his lips. "Harper is my only child. What do you mean how many children do they think I have?"

"Oh, I was just wondering since Harper is the third child to disappear in this exact manner in less than two weeks. I can't imagine they think you've taken others as well..." She left her last sentence open waiting for what she said to sink in.

Melinda started crying and turned on Travis. "How could you do this to me?" She got up and ran into her bedroom. She laid on her stomach, clutching her pillow to her face.

Travis excused himself and went after her. He sat on the side of the bed and rested his hand on her back. She stirred enough to tell him to stop but he didn't. "Melinda, I didn't do anything. You have to understand the police are just trying to do their job. I didn't even know that other babies were missing. I'm not happy that they questioned me but I was able to prove to them that I was home last night. As soon as I did that, they left. And they never asked me about any other children."

She picked up her head just enough so her words weren't muffled in the pillow. "But why would they question you at all if they didn't think you did anything wrong? Did you get another woman pregnant and not tell me?" She started crying again, harder this time.

"No, Melinda, I told you. They were just doing their job. Besides, I really hate to say this right now but... I didn't even want Harper. Why would I go out and get a second woman pregnant, or a third for that matter?"

Leila hit the pause button on her recorder and tiptoed out of the apartment. Now she had a story to write.

Chapter IV

They saw her in her most vulnerable state. Her guard was let down. It was the perfect opportunity to take what they wanted.

Dixie and Rock were finishing up their paperwork and planning on heading home for the evening. Dixie had just saved her last report when, from inside Stone's office, they heard his cell phone ring, his desk phone ring, and his email chime. Dixie threw her head back and sighed. "Maybe we're not leaving tonight."

Stone came out of his office and sat on top of the desk across from them. He appeared calm and that worried both of them. He laid his palms together and pressed his fingers to his lips. "I like to believe that I have two competent, trust worthy detectives working for me. Sometimes, though, you make it really hard for me and I can't keep making excuses for you without also making myself look incompetent." His eyes darted back and forth between the two of them but neither of them spoke. "No comment from either of you?"

Rock sat up straight in his chair. "Maybe it would help if you filled us in on what you're talking about."

Dixie nodded in agreement.

"A few days ago, you informed me that Leila Romero was poking her nose around and trying to get an interview from the first two mothers.

Now, you would think, knowing she's working the story, a competent detective would tell any new witnesses, victims, or suspects not to talk to any reporters. But, apparently, my detectives don't think about things like that and decide it's okay for both a victim and a potential suspect to talk to one."

"Wait a minute? Who talked to her?"

Stone pressed his lips together and furrowed his brow. "Melinda and her ex-friend slash baby daddy. It gets better though, because all the information we had kept confidential so far, you know, all the information we had that could tie the victims together, single moms, baby ages, that sort of thing? That's all out on the internet now because the two of them told her everything she needed to know."

Rock had his eyes turned up toward the ceiling and Dixie's mouth was hanging open.

"You two want to hear the best part? Pay attention because this is a good one. Somehow, while Leila was interviewing them, she managed to pit them against each other and led Melinda to believe that her baby's daddy had not just the one child with her, but two other babies with two other women at the same time."

"What?" Rock and Dixie said in unison.

"That's right. In print, and electronically, it is now stated that Travis not only fathered Melinda's baby but also Brenda's and Chrissy's. And he went on the record with the following," he grabbed the piece of paper he had walked out of his office with and snapped it in the air, "I didn't even want [name extracted], why would I go out and get two other women pregnant?"

"Fucking Christ!" Rock bellowed and slammed his fist on his desk. "If it wasn't illegal, I'd strangle Leila. I may do it anyway."

Dixie rested her head in her open palm. "Oh, this isn't good."

"So, my very competent detectives, how are you going to fix this one?" Stone slid off the desk and walked casually back to his office.

The entire station was so quiet all anyone could hear was the buzzing of the overhead lights.

"Fuck!" Rock yelled again and Dixie, along with half the remaining people in the office, jumped.

"So, you want to grab a drink before heading home?" She raised her eyebrows at him.

"After you."

They both drove their own cars and met at the same bar they had gone to a little more than a week ago. When they walked in the bartender pointed to a back table and they saw Gemini sitting in a booth with her head back and her eyes closed. Rock held up two fingers and the bartender nodded.

"Hey, gorgeous. Hope you don't mind if we join you." Rock slid onto the bench next to Gemini.

"I'd be insulted if you didn't. Hey, Dixie."

"Hi. I hope you had a more productive day than we did."

"That depends on what you consider productive. If you mean, did my team manage to take every single star off Brenda's ceiling, then yes, it was productive. What a nightmare that was. I left after two hours, we had barely made a dent."

"I guess that means you didn't find any fingerprints for us yet, huh?" Rock curled up the corner of his lips.

Gemini laughed. "My poor techs couldn't feel their arms after having them raised for so long."

"Thank you," Rock said when the bartender placed two beers on the table.

"So, no luck for you guys either?"

Dixie shook her head. "Not unless you count the newest mother and her ex talking to a reporter as luck."

"Oh, shit. Stone must be pissed."

Rock nodded. "You could say that. I'm not sure if you're aware but you're talking to two of the most incompetent detectives to ever roam the Earth."

"That was his argument? What are you supposed to do? Handcuff them to a cabinet and duct tape their mouths shut?"

"Apparently."

They were all quiet, listening to the music, enjoying their drinks.

"So, Dixie? Not that you haven't been asked a thousand times before but..."

"How'd I get my name?"

Gemini nodded and smiled.

"A thousand and one now. I wish I had some kind of fun story for it but I don't. The song Dixie Road was really popular the year I was born and my mother loved it." She rolled her eyes. "She thought she was being cute since my last name is Lane." She laughed at the look on Gemini's face. "Yup. Instead of Dixie Road, I got Dixie Lane."

Gemini laughed out loud. "That is classic. I almost want to give her credit for it except for the fact that it's...well, it's a terrible story for you to have to tell people."

"Right? The worst part is, I've tried for years to come up with a good story and I can't even think of one." She took a sip of her beer. "What about you? Your name is pretty unusual, too."

"I have a story. Short and sad. I have a twin who died three minutes after she was born. I was delivered twenty minutes later. My mom is one of those spiritual type people and believed from the beginning that my sister's soul became part of me. So, Gemini."

"Wow. That's short and kind of beautiful, actually."

"Yeah. It's a nice thought. And it makes my mom happy to believe part of my sister lives on in me."

"Were you identical?" Rock asked the question as if he'd been a part of the conversation the entire time.

"Yeah, we were."

"There could have been two of you walking around, huh?" He nudged Gemini's arm with his elbow.

"There almost was. But I don't think the world could have handled two of me."

"The world? No. But I could have handle one of you. I mean, you're like my sister but she would be..."

"She would still be like your sister, you pig. We were identical. Every time you looked at her you would see me." She slapped him in the arm with the back of her hand and all three of them fell into a fit of laughter.

Crude as it may have been, they all needed that bit of humor. Dixie could see the love Rock and Gemini had for each other and it made her happy to see them bicker back and forth.

Before they got to the bar, Rock had taken it upon himself to text his wife to let her know he would be home soon. He backed into his driveway and turned on the dash cam like he had been instructed to do. He wasn't going to allow Stone to watch his house so he gave him a nice view of the street instead. He walked through the door just as Jill was putting food on the table.

"I thought you might be hungry." She shrugged and walked over to give him a hug.

He wrapped his arms around her and felt the stress roll off his body. He stayed in that position until he felt her ease her grasp.

"You had a tough day, didn't you?" She retrieved a beer and a bottle of water from the refrigerator before sitting down. When he didn't respond she said, "I saw the article."

"Oh." He stuffed a fork full of mashed potatoes into his mouth. "Yeah, that was not a good way to end the work day. Stone is pissed. He's trying to blame it on us because people don't know when to keep their mouths shut. So, tomorrow morning, I get to go have a nice, friendly chat with Leila. You know how much I like that."

Jill nodded her head. "She's an awful woman. Doesn't she know she's ruining people's lives with the stuff she writes?"

"I don't think she cares."

"But, as a woman, you would think she'd have more compassion."

"Even with her being a writer, I don't think she knows what that word means. She's single and bitter and I think she relishes in being able to make other people as miserable as she is."

After dinner, Jill washed the dishes and cleaned up the kitchen while Rock spent some time with Ella. He put her to bed and went in to take a long, hot shower. When he got out, he found Jill already curled up under the blankets. He slid in beside her and wrapped his body around her. She stirred and pushed back against him before rolling over to face him. He ran his fingertips down her spine, kissing her deeply before pulling her on top of him.

Rock grunted when he rolled over. His picked up his phone and saw Stone's name running across the screen. "Rockefeller."

"Go outside, you have a note."

"Captain, it's three in the morning. Can't it wait?"

"That wasn't a request."

"Fine. I'll call you back."

"Nope. Take me with you. And bring your gun, they could still be out there."

Rock grumbled and slipped out of bed. He grabbed the pants he wore the previous day and did his best to put them on with one hand without falling over. He didn't bother trying to fasten his belt. With his free hand, he pulled back the curtain in his bedroom window and glanced outside, keeping his back to the wall. He grabbed his gun off his nightstand and slid it into his waistband. Before opening the front door, he performed the same act in the living room window, checking his surroundings so he didn't get attacked when he walked outside. Keeping his back to the house, the cement walkway was cold under his bare feet.

Stone was still talking into the phone and Rock was doing his best to tune him out so he could listen for any signs that someone else was still lurking. He took one more look around before stepping out of the full cover of shadows. Like so many previous events, the note was tucked neatly under his driver's windshield wiper. Dropping his phone on the passenger seat, he grabbed two latex gloves from his glove box and wrestled to get them on in his state of being half asleep. He heard Stone's voice as he put the phone back to his ear.

"What's it say?"

"I didn't get it yet. But I'm guessing you know that since you can see me walking around the front of my car. So creepy, Captain." He took the note from the windshield and stepped into the street to utilize the light from the street lamp.

"Ha," was all Rock could manage to get out.

"Waiting."

"Captain, did you see someone leave the note?"

"As our luck goes, I stepped away for two minutes. I came back and it was there. I haven't replayed the tape yet. Why?"

Rock laughed and was thankful he lived in a quiet neighborhood where everyone minded their business. He knew he would look insane to anyone who happened to look out their window right now. "It says, 'Your camera won't help you.'"

"Son of a bitch."

"I'm going to go back to sleep now. I'll drop this off at the lab before I head in." He ended the call, bagged the note, and made sure to lock his door before going back to his bed. He laid down and stared at the ceiling for the next three hours before his alarm told him to get up.

Rock took a cool shower to wake himself up, changed Ella, gave her a bottle, and laid her in her bassinet. Even though he had barely slept, he thought Jill deserved to sleep in for a while. Before leaving his house, he gently kissed her forehead.

She whispered, "love you," and rolled over, instantly falling back to sleep.

Rock dropped the note off at the lab and stopped at the small coffee shop a few blocks from the station to pick up a coffee for himself and Dixie. He was exhausted and already dreading the day that he knew would prove to be pure hell. He doubted he'd even be able to sit down before Stone called him into his office and he had to go see Leila which always put him in a sour mood.

He slid the coffee on the desk in front of Dixie.

She looked up at him and smiled. "I think I love you." She wrapped her hands around the cup as if to warm them.

The corners of Rock's lips twitched. "Most women do."

"You're obnoxious."

"No. If I actually believed it, that would be obnoxious. How was your night?"

"Not bad. I got about five hours of sleep. Yours?"

Rock sat in his chair, rested his feet on the top of his desk, and yawned. "You should ask Stone. We had a nice chat at three o'clock this morning."

"Oh, no. What happened?"

Rock stared at her for a minute and for the first time, noticed how beautiful she was. Her straight blond hair rested just on the tops of her shoulders, one side tucked neatly behind her ear. Like her stature, her features were small but vibrant. Her eyes were almond shaped with an almost neon blue coloring and her lips were full and pouting. Her outfit from the day before, which caught his attention, changed the way he looked at her. Now, with her sitting there, waiting for an answer, her lips were calling to him, inviting him over. He knew it was wrong but he couldn't stop thinking about it. "Uhh. My friend came back and left a note on my car. I'm pretty sure Stone sat there and watched that damn camera all night long."

"A new one already? I thought you said it was only every few weeks? What'd it say?"

Rock couldn't help but laugh. From a logical standpoint, he knew it was anything but funny but the words just got to him. "It said my camera wouldn't help me."

Dixie's eyes widened. "And why is that funny?"

"Just because, the whole point in putting it there was for it to be hidden. It was the thing that was supposed to help us catch whoever it is. Apparently, they're either smarter than we want to give them credit for or they really are following me everywhere I go. Either way, we have to give credit where credit is due and they're pretty good at what they're doing."

Rock spent the next hour performing his usual morning routine and was pleasantly surprised that Stone came in, greeted them, and went silently to his office. If only every day could start that well. "All right, I need to go have a chat with Leila. I'm going to see if I can catch her before she heads out to try to ruin our case more than she already has. Coming?"

Dixie didn't need any convincing. She more than happy to go watch Rock give her an ear full. Plus, she didn't want to stay behind and risk the possibility of Stone coming out and trying to chat with her.

They settled in the car and Rock asked Dixie to call Melinda to check in on her. He wanted to know exactly what happened the day before and why she talked to Leila. He was annoyed by the one sided conversation and drummed his fingers on the steering wheel while he waited to hear the other side of it once Dixie hung up.

"Well, I guess we have some sort of answer."

"And the answer being?"

"Melinda said Leila told her she was working with us. That's why she let her in. And, you're going to love this part. Leila followed Melinda and Travis to their bedroom and printed pieces of their personal conversation... without their permission."

Rock laughed at the absurdity of the last statement. "She really is a piece of work, that one. Vicious as they come."

He found a spot directly outside the news station. Dixie opened her door and he placed his hand on her arm to stop her from getting out. "We're going to wait here for her to come out. We'll extend a professional courtesy to her that she seems to forget exists."

"How adult of you." She sat back in her seat and closed her door again. "Kind of wish you would have told me though. I would have used the bathroom before we left."

"Typical. Oh, and we have perfect timing." Rock scurried out of the car and Dixie almost had to run to catch up with him. "Leila?"

She turned toward him and rolled her eyes. "What do you want? I'm in a hurry."

"What do you think I want? I want you to stop leaking information that we haven't approved."

"Detective Rockefeller, I'm sure I don't have to tell you that I don't need your permission to print anything. I don't work for you. If people give me the information, I'm allowed to write it."

"That's true, but you also know you're hurting our case and making our chances of finding the perp smaller when you print stuff that shouldn't be public knowledge."

"Well, now. You can't blame me for doing my job well just because you seem to have trouble doing yours."

Rock threw his arm straight out and stopped Dixie in her tracks, almost knocking her backwards.

"Down, girl. If you're good, I'll bring you a bone later. Would you like that?" She grinned and narrowed her eyes. "Good luck, Detectives." She turned and strutted away.

Dixie could feel the stress beginning to pull her down. She needed an outlet and having a drink after work wasn't quite enough to calm her down. She made a call to an old friend who promised to stop. With a few hours to spare, she made herself dinner, took a shower and applied fresh makeup to her face. She sat curled up on the couch, reading a book, and was about to fall asleep when she heard the knock at her door. She opened it just wide enough to see who was there.

He stood there long enough for her to recognize that it was him before pushing through the door and spinning her around. He slid a cloth covering over her eyes and pulled her arms tight behind her back. Dixie screeched and he leaned forward and whispered in her ear. "Shh. You don't want your neighbors to hear us, do you?" He kicked the door closed with the heel of his boot and prodded her toward the bedroom. Using his knees, he pressed her thighs against the bed, holding her in place. He reached around her and unbuttoned her pants, sliding his hands into her waistband and eased her pants down. He ran his hands from the back of her knees up to her spine where he pressed gently, guiding her torso onto the bed. He reached into her nightstand, holding her in place again and pulled out her favorite toy. He brought his arm back and swung it forward hitting one cheek perfectly center with the flogger.

Dixie cried out from the sweet mix of pleasure and pain and rose up on the balls of her feet which signified she was asking for more. He complied and relished in the snapping sounds of each strand making contact with her skin. Dixie moaned in response. She stepped out of her pants and he gently nudged her to climb up on the bed on all fours. He kneeled behind her and gathered her hair in the palm of his hand, pulling her head back. "I'm enjoying how obedient you're being tonight. Does that mean you want me to keep going?"

"Yes, please, Master," she whined.

"I thought so." He brought his hand down and spanked her hard before slipping inside her.

Dixie showered again and climbed in to bed feeling satiated and much more relaxed. He always knew exactly what she needed and how much. She had just drifted off to sleep when her phone rang on her nightstand. She sat up and squinted, trying to read the screen. "Shit," she grumbled. "This is Lane."

She dressed, professionally this time, and hopped in her car, thankful she was only going a few blocks into the city. When she arrived, not seeing Rock's car anywhere, she sat back in her seat and closed her eyes, hoping for a quick cat nap before he got there. She had barely entered a serene state when a knock on her window startled her back to reality.

"Rise and shine, sweetheart. We got ourselves a kidnapping case to solve."

"I haven't slept yet." She stepped out of her car and almost fell into Rock.

"Never would have guessed." He placed his hand on the back of her elbow and guided her toward the apartment building. "Four days again."

"Four days what?" She shook her head, trying to wake herself up.

"Since the last call. Each one has come in exactly four days after the last."

They walked in to the apartment and, as usual, the mother was taking to a uniformed officer. They walked past without stopping to say anything and proceeded to the nursery. Dixie walked in first and stopped abruptly. Rock slammed into the back of her and caught her before she toppled forward.

"What was that about?"

"Little. Miss. Muffet."

"Oh, don't start again. I can't..."

"No, it's Little Miss Muffet." She pointed to a pink, velveteen ottoman in the middle of the floor with a stuffed spider sitting on top. "Those are the clues we haven't figured out yet. Little Miss Muffet. Three Little Kittens. Twinkle, Twinkle Little Star."

Rock stared at the ottoman. "We need you to not sleep more often. Now, while you're at it. What do the nursery rhymes mean and what's with the bingo balls?"

In her excitement, she had forgotten all about the bingo balls. Not having an answer for them, she ignored the question.

This was the first nursery they had been in with curtains hanging from the window. The floor was carpeted and the walls were adorned with a floral wallpaper. Rock and Dixie were busy looking at the dresser when they heard what sounded like wood cracking behind them. They turned around to see an officer half-sitting in a rocking chair in the corner. The buzz of voices had suddenly gone silent. Rock's face grew serious and he shouted. "Out. Now. And leave your badge number."

"I'm sorry, I..."

"OUT!" His voice echoed through the apartment.

No one in the room dared move until Rock gave them permission to do so. Even Dixie stood still and had to remind herself that it was okay to breathe. Rock was practicing a deep breathing exercise that he had found useful when he was about to go off the wall. Once he felt a bit calmer, he opened his eyes and could feel everyone staring at him. He stepped forward and crouched down. "At least he found the bingo ball."

There was a collective mumbling throughout the nursery and people began to move around again.

"Kiersten? Do you mind answering a few questions for me?" Dixie told Rock to go take a minute outside when she saw how upset he still was. She had offered to do the interview and he was more than happy to walk away for a while.

"I don't mind. But I'm not sure how much I'll be able to help you." Like the others, she was wearing a tank top and lounge pants. Kiersten still had on a full face of makeup, almost like she hadn't slept at all yet.

"You might be more help than you think. Sometimes, even what seems like the most insignificant of details is what helps us solve the case. Just be as honest as you can, okay?"

Kiersten nodded and sat on a bar stool that was against the kitchen counter.

"Can you walk me through what you did last night? Around the time you were putting Cassidy to bed?" Dixie grabbed a second stool and pulled it around to the end of the bar counter.

"It was about nine o'clock. I went in to my room to change my clothes. I was still wearing what I had worn to work. I came back out and fed Cassidy and then laid her in her crib. I don't sing, she'd have nightmares for life, for sure, but I read her a bedtime story."

"What story did you read?"

"Um. Goodnight Moon." Her eyes glassed over at the thought of reading to her daughter. "By the time I finished the book she wasn't fully asleep, so I started it again. After a few pages, I set it on the dresser and walked out. Normally I would shower before I went to bed but I was so tired. I laid down and read about three pages of my own book before I drifted off."

"Keep going," Dixie nudged.

"Well, I woke up at about two. I was actually startled awake."

"What startled you? Did you hear a noise or...?"

"No, at least I don't think so. Honestly, I think I woke up because I had slept for nearly four hours. I don't know if you have any children, Detective, but that's about unheard of when you have an infant. It's almost like my brain told me there was something wrong because it's wasn't used to relaxing for so long. Anyway, I jumped out of bed and practically ran into the nursery and Cassidy was gone."

"Aside from her missing, did you notice anything else that was different? A smell, an object, something moved within the nursery."

She thought about it for a minute before answering. "Nothing was moved. I did see the spider but that wasn't until after I called the police." She let out a nervous laugh. "You want to know how stupid I am? I was still partly sleeping and I was scared and maybe in somewhat of a state of shock. I actually looked for her. I looked under her crib, I pulled out the dresser drawers, I checked the couch and the closets thinking maybe I had set her somewhere that I didn't mean to. Have you ever done something like that? Like, put your keys in the freezer and spent hours looking for them?" She laughed again, unintentionally, through the tears that were now welling up in her eyes.

Dixie smiled and rested her hand on top of Kiersten's. "I think we've all done that. But you're need to find your daughter doesn't make you stupid, it makes you human. She was missing and you were trying to find her. That's an excellent quality to have as a mother." Dixie was hoping her reassurance would make Kiersten feel better but she only cried harder.

"What kind of quality is it that would make a mother put her own newborn in a dresser drawer? Or, at least think she did?"

"The protective kind. Deep down, you knew she wasn't in there, but your motherly instinct to protect her made you search anywhere you could to try to find her and keep her safe." She gave Kiersten a few minutes to calm herself down before asking her next round of questions.

"Is Cassidy's father still a part of your life?"

She shook her head weakly. "I don't know who he is. I went out with some friends for a girl's night and ended up inviting some guy over here. I think it goes without saying that alcohol was involved. We, um, well, you know. We had sex and when I woke up in the morning, he was gone."

"Did you get his name? His phone number? Anything?"

Kiersten was hesitant to answer. "Nothing. For some reason, I didn't think he would just disappear. I really can be stupid sometimes. I think his name was Michael or Mitch. Maybe Matthew. But that's all I've got."

"Did your friends get his name or did any of you get any pictures of him or of the two of you together?"

"I asked them months ago when I found out I was pregnant. No one remembers a thing about that night."

Rock walked back inside with Gemini and her team. He looked much better than he did when he walked out the door and Dixie guessed he had been able to vent to Gemini. Rock was much more lenient with uniformed officers than Dixie had ever been and she was struggling to get used to it. Back in Georgia, the uniformed cops were there strictly to control entry and begin the interview with basic questions which they passed on to the detectives as soon as they got there. Once the detectives and/or forensics team was on site, the uniforms filed out without being prompted to do so. Surprisingly, Rock allowed them to trample all over the crime scene. She had asked him about it on the first night and he told her it wasn't a priority for him. Now, after the officer thought it was a good idea to sit down, potentially destroying, contaminating, or erasing evidence, maybe she would be able to convince him that it was a bad idea to allow them to stay. She could only hope.

Gemini touched the back of her arm lightly. "Good work with the nursery rhyme clues. It seems so obvious now that we have an answer."

Dixie nodded her head in agreement. "I know. It hit me all at once. We should have seen it with the little mittens."

By nine in the morning, the nurses were huddled around the computer monitor all trying to read the latest article from Leila Romero. More than anything, the headline was what caught their attention.

FOURTH INFANT GOES MISSING; POLICE STILL CLUELESS

It was obvious to all of them that Leila had not gotten to speak to the victim of this one yet but she was clearly not happy with how the detectives were doing their job. In so many words, she ranted about how useless they were and how she had been able to get more information about the case than they did, although she failed to provide any additional information than her previous article contained.

All the nurses were commiserating about what the police knew and didn't know and wondered how a reporter was getting more information than they were. Shaina spoke up and reminded them that the police had to keep information confidential in order to bait people into admitting they knew facts that weren't made public.

"All I'm saying is that there's a reason reporters and police don't get along. One needs to hide the information in order to do their job and the other needs to give the information in order to do theirs. One of them is always going to win. In this case, they happened to get the one reporter that will stop at nothing to get her story. I'm guessing you all didn't read the article that

Captain Stone approved a few days ago for the City Gazette. He basically came right out and called Leila a liar. Apparently, some of the information she printed in her last article was taken out of context and was supposed to be off the record. But, she's a sly one."

Julie couldn't stay quiet any more. "I really hate to be that person but are you seriously siding with the police right now? Four infants, four, have now disappeared and it doesn't seem like they're any closer to finding out who's taking them. You can't seriously believe they are doing their jobs efficiently."

"I do. What if there really aren't any clues? What if they're so obscure they haven't figured them out yet? Solving cases takes time whether we want to believe it or not." She turned away and left the room without another word.

Rock slammed the printed version of the article on the desk. "Vicious, that's all she is. I don't know if someone didn't love her enough as a child or if she really longs for attention that much. But this is ridiculous. Every word of this article is complete bullshit. I can almost guarantee she wrote it to get back at Stone for calling her a liar the other day. The only good thing about this one is that she didn't give away any more details. I'm so glad Kiersten is competent and hasn't spoken to her. Speaking of, were you able to get a hold of any of her friends that she went out with that night?"

"Only one." Dixie looked through her notebook. "Her friend named Maggie. She said she remembers Kiersten getting friendly with the guy after he sat next to her at the bar but they didn't stay much longer after that. Kiersten said not to worry about giving her a ride home and she left with him. According to Maggie, they were all pretty messed up and she doubts if anyone else will be able to provide any more information. One of them was supposed to be the designated driver but they ended up taking a taxi home because none of them were able to drive. It doesn't help us with any bit of our case but at least they were responsible. We have to give them credit for that."

Rock just rolled his eyes. "I don't think we need to give them credit for being responsible adults but maybe that's just me." He finally sat down and looked calmer than he had in hours. "This is great. We've had zero luck with the men so far and this time we don't even have one to question."

"That's true. But we also have our first reliable mother. She's honest, at least so far, and she gives coherent answers."

"That's the least we could ask for." Rock went into a storage room and brought out a map of the city that he pinned to the back of their white board. "Let's see if we can find a connection to all these places."

Dixie read off the addresses while Rock placed a marker for each one. While they both hoped not to have to add any more places, having only four didn't prove to show any kind of pattern. "Well, that didn't help much, did it?"

"Not as far as I can tell now." He strung a piece of yarn twice, across the markers to see where they intersected. "Let's pull up a digital map and see where they intersect. At least maybe that will give us something to go check out."

Where the yarn intersected was small city block with a bar, a convenience store, a Chinese food restaurant, a dry cleaner, and a tiny cafe. Apartments were located above the businesses and in most instances, were usually occupied by the business owners. It was mid-morning by the time they made it to their destination. Summer had begun to make an appearance and the sun's rays were burning into the fabric of their jackets. The cool breeze was the only thing that made the heat tolerable.

They started with the businesses, asking basic questions about their patrons and if they had seen anyone suspicious. The convenience store and the cafe owners laughed when they were asked that question.

"Detectives, we're not exactly in the best part of town. Almost every person we see is suspicious."

Being in the city, almost every business owner and resident had been conditioned to play dumb. None of them were strangers to having their day interrupted by detectives or police officers. Their answers were almost always the same and were some combination of: *I don't know anything. I didn't see anything. I didn't hear anything. I'm in a hurry, are we done here?* It didn't make their job any easier but every once in a while they got lucky and found someone who was willing to take the time to talk to them.

Today, they did not have any such luck. None of the business owners could give them any useful information. They made two trips to the apartments above the businesses. The second round was made after five when they figured most of the residents they missed would be home from work. There were a lot of single tenants but none who had had a child recently and the majority of them were men. Rock wondered if maybe that what they were looking for. Not for their next victim but the perpetrator putting himself directly in their sight without their knowledge.

When they got back to the station, he gave half the list of resident's names to Dixie. "I want to look at the criminal backgrounds of all the men."

"Why?"

"Because. The only thing we have to go on right now are the places where the infants have been taken. We don't have any sort of definitive pattern and there aren't any infants in that central area. So maybe, it's not the next victim we're looking for. Maybe it's the perp."

"Oh. Because they can't stay to watch us work, they have to draw us to them."

"Exactly."

Rock asked Gemini to meet him at the bar. He wanted to go home and spend some time with his wife but he wasn't quite ready to do so. Gemini had had an insanely busy day and was more than happy to accept his invitation.

The two chatted about work and Gemini practiced her best stalling techniques while fighting the urge to ask Rock how he was doing, emotionally, with the case. After a solid forty-five minutes, she couldn't wait any longer.

"Rock, enough about the case details. How are you holding up?" She put her hand up to interrupt him before he could reply. "I know you're going to get annoyed with me and tell me you're fine. I get that part. But you're four kids into this case now. It has to be taking its toll on you." Her eyes were pleading with him to answer her honestly.

He played with the edge of the napkin under his drink and sighed heavily. "It is. I don't want to admit it, but it is. I know it sounds awful but the last two times I've gotten a call, I've had a split second of being thankful. Because if it was someone else's child, it means it wasn't mine. All the calls have been coming in at about the same time and every night I've been getting up around one and sleeping in her room until three of four in the morning just to make sure no one else comes in. It's crazy. I'm not a paranoid person, I don't ever let things get to me. But I'm terrified every time I leave my house. I'm afraid every time I'm home but not in the same room as Ella. Jesus, I carry her around with me like a little girl would carry around her baby doll. The worst part though, is that my wife notices. She sees that I won't let Ella out of my sight. She's already called me out on it on more than one occasion. It's actually putting a strain on our marriage. I'm sure it may be hard to believe, but it's true."

"Actually, I can believe it. Granted, I don't have a child or even a significant other, but I think I can understand the thought process behind it. Is that why you've been putting off going home?"

"Mostly, yes. Every day I can't wait to go home and at the same time, I dread doing exactly that. It's like no matter what I do, I can't relax."

"I'm going to tell you a few things that you already know but I want you to listen anyway. The first is that this is exactly why some officers can't cut it in this business. It's not just one case that makes them feel this way, it's all of them. The second thing is, you're not alone. Cases that involve children effect people at a much higher rate than those that involve adults. Third, you do have the option to step away if need be. Don't interrupt me. I know you won't, I'm just reminding you that it is an option. Fourth, and last, you do have specialists that you can talk to if for no other reason, than to vent your frustrations. It is possible they may be able to provide some pointers to you for how to cope with such a case that is more personal than you're used to. That was it, I'm done being your guide."

"I suppose I should say 'thank you'?"

"You don't need to. You said it by listening to what I was telling you." Gemini stood and leaned forward to kiss him on the cheek. "I'm here for you, Rock. Any time you need to talk." She walked away before he could reply to her.

Rock stayed and had two more drinks before getting up enough nerve to go home. It was a little after eight and he was hoping he might be able to get some quality time in with Ella before she went to bed and with his wife before she got too mad at him for staying out too late. When he backed in to his driveway, he sat in his car for a moment and collected all of his belongings. One way or another, he was going to find a way to keep his family safe.

The following morning, Rock was greeted by a large envelope stuffed under his windshield wiper with a note taped to the back.

Let's play a game entitled
"Who knows your partner best?"

Do you know where she went last night,
When she should have gone home to rest?

Do you think she put up a solid fight,
Or is this just her way?

Focus on your objective,
Have you talked to her today?

Pain or pleasure, detective?
Keep your eyes on the clock.

Don't allow yourself to be idled,
Tick tock... tick tock.

He pulled a Swiss army knife from his front pocket and carefully cut the envelope at the bottom seam, not wanting to destroy any possible evidence. Inside, he found a stack of photos, each more graphic than the last. The first, a photo of someone's hands, handcuffed to a bed frame. The next, a back view of a female bending over, red welts covering her skin. A woman's chest, scratch marks embedded in her cleavage. Raised bite marks on a woman's torso. A female's head, only from the blindfold up. And the last one, a photo showing the woman from her neck down, completely exposed. Raw, red, and swollen.

"What the hell?" Rock jumped in his car and looked at the note one more time before calling Dixie. Sweat beaded on his forehead and he heard his blood rushing in his ears. He bounced the heel of his foot and drummed his fingers on the steering wheel while hitting the 'call' button for the third time. "Detective Lane. I can't get to my phone right now..."

Chapter V

This women was ruining their plan. They would have to find a way to remove her before she caused real trouble.

Rock ended the call and his tires squealed as he left his driveway. He instinctively headed toward Dixie's house, cursing her for living so far away. While he was waiting at a red light he shot off a quick text asking if she was okay and told her to call him as soon as possible. He entered the expressway and forced his way to the left lane before calling Stone.

"I need you to send patrol over to Dixie's. If she's not at the station when you get there, I need you to come out to her place, too. I'm on my way there now."

"Whoa, slow down. Why are we sending cars out to her house?"

"I got a new note and photos from the person who's watching me. She may be in trouble."

"What kind of trouble and where are you now?"

"She may be hurt if the photos are genuine. Her phone is going straight to voicemail. I just got on the expressway."

"Okay. I'm on my way to the station, patrol is on their way to her house. You go to the lab and bring Gemini what you have. If Dixie really is in trouble, let's get all the information to Gemini as soon as we can."

He sighed and jerked his wheel over so he could make the next exit. The blare of the horn from the car behind him made him jump. "Just...when you get in, let me know if she's okay. I'll be there soon." He hung up before Stone could say anything else.

He pulled into the parking lot of the lab ten minutes later and ran inside. "I need Gemini, now." The security guard, knowing Rock as he did, didn't question him and immediately picked up the phone to page her.

The main door opened and she poked her head out. "Rock? Something wrong?"

He thrust the evidence bag full of pictures and the note into her hand. "I have an envelope, a note, and pictures. I'm warning you, you may not be impressed."

She flipped the bag over in her hand so she could read the note. Her face paled and she looked slowly over to Rock. "Dixie?"

"I don't know if it's her or not. I've called her phone numerous times. It keeps going right to her voicemail."

Gemini, having pulled on a pair of gloves, looked at the first picture. "Well, call her right now." She continued looking through the photos while Rock tried Dixie's cell phone again.

"Voicemail."

"Try the station."

Rock's heart pounded in his chest and his thumbs fumbled over the buttons on his phone screen. He felt helpless as the phone rang for the second time. He heard the click of the receiver and felt a rush of hopeful relief course over is body.

"Detective Lane."

"Oh, Dixie. Are you okay?"

Gemini looked up briefly and could see the concern leave his face. She continued going through the pictures.

"I'm fine, why?"

"I just wanted to hear your voice to be sure."

Dixie laughed into her phone. "I'm sorry. That just sounds so odd coming from your mouth. Why wouldn't I be okay?"

Gemini waved her hand in the air to get Rock's attention and started motioning for him to give her his phone.

"Uh, hold on just a second, okay?" He handed his phone over and furrowed his brow.

"Dixie? Hey, it's Gemini. Listen, I know how weird this is going to sound to you but it's really important." She turned so she was facing away from Rock. "Do you have any tattoos?"

"What has gotten into you two this morning? Are you both okay?"

"It's important. Please, just answer the question."

"Uh, yeah. I have one."

"Where is it and what is it of?"

"I don't see... never mind, I won't argue with you. I have one. It's a tiny orchid on my hip. Now, can you tell me what this is all about?"

"Are you sure you're okay, like physically?"

"Aside from my perpetual state of exhaustion, I'm fine."

"Okay. Do me a favor and turn your phone on. Rock and Stone have been trying to reach you all morning."

Dixie pulled her cell out of her pocket and looked at the screen. "My phone is on. I haven't gotten any calls or messages all morning."

"Huh. Let me finish up here with Rock and he can fill you in when he gets there. Don't go anywhere." She heard Dixie begin to protest but she ended the call anyway. She turned back to face Rock and flipped a photo around for him to see. It was the most explicit. "She swears she fine. This," she pointed to the hip in the photograph, "is a tattoo she actually has."

Rock rubbed his forehead, wiping the remaining bit of sweat from his brow. "I didn't even notice that when I looked through them. I guess the anxiety of having something hit so close affected me more than I thought. And it's going only to get better. I can't believe you left me in a position to explain this to her. You couldn't have offered to do it?"

Gemini blinked at him slowly. "I can either go with you to talk to her or I can get started looking for fingerprints and maybe DNA from this envelope."

Rock's phone rang and he looked at the screen. "Shit. I'm going to have to tell Stone, too."

"I might suggest not doing it over the phone. Wait until you get in."

He thought about it for a moment and sent him a text instead.

Talked to Dixie. She's at the station.

"You know he's going to call you next."

Gemini nodded. "I can handle Stone. You get to the station and I'll get started with these." She flapped the photos and envelope in the air.

"You know I appreciate you."

"I'll call you." She turned and walked away and Rock headed to the station.

Stone called Rock three more times while he was driving and he sent each to voicemail. He sat in the parking lot of the station, hesitant to go in, until he knew he couldn't wait any longer. He had to walk directly past Dixie to get to Stone's office and as bad as he felt for making her wait even longer, he knew there was a chain of command that he had to follow.

He walked through the door of the station with his head down and as he approached Dixie, he held up his finger and uttered, "Give me just a minute," before entering Stone's office and closing the door behind him.

"What is going on?" Stone looked pissed and Rock didn't blame him. "I know it's important if Gemini wouldn't even tell me."

Rock fought back a smile and sat across the desk from Stone. He owed Gemini for her loyalty. "Like I told you, I got a note and some pictures on my windshield. The note made reference to 'my partner' and the photos were kind of graphic."

"I didn't even look at the footage yet and I wasn't watching because I didn't expect a new note so soon. Did the person actually threaten Dixie?"

"Mmm. Not exactly." He took out his phone and showed him the pictures that Gemini had scanned and texted to him. He hated having possession of them in any capacity but Stone needed to see them. "Gemini spoke to her while I was there this morning. She confirmed, without prompting, that she has that exact tattoo. God, I hate having these on my phone. I feel like I'm completely invading her privacy."

"It's not you that's doing it. It's whoever is watching you. They're trying to prove to you that they really can see you. They know who your partner is, they have information they shouldn't have. They're trying to tell you they're a real threat and not some harmless prank."

The two sat in silence for a moment and then Stone cleared his throat. "Damn. It feels so inappropriate to have to tell her this. Maybe Gemini will..."

"I tried. She's busy."

"Maybe if I call her?"

"With all due respect, Captain, she wouldn't even tell you why I was there this morning."

"Fine. Let's just get this over with."

Dixie and Rock sat across from each other, in uncomfortable silence, all day. He had apologized numerous times but she wasn't entertaining any of it. He didn't blame her and was trying not to take it personally. Not only did the person violating her privacy learn her secrets, but because of their profession, Rock was required to show not one, but two other people. He was mad when Stone forced him to put a camera in his car and that was only showing the street he lived in. With Dixie, it not only showed her, but also the most private moments in her life. Without her saying anything, he couldn't tell whether she was upset, angry, or embarrassed. He could only guess it was most likely not the latter.

Rock had three more meetings in Stone's office before the day was over. Because the circumstances with Dixie were connected to the incident that was already in progress with Rock, Stone had to contact people a few links higher in the chain of command. As far as he could tell, Stone was cooperative and answered all their questions as honestly as he was able. When they asked him to forward the evidence he had, he put his foot down and outwardly refused to do so, stating it was a violation of privacy and he would turn it over if and when it became absolutely necessary and not a moment before. Stone's stance on that matter allowed Rock to gain a new found respect for his captain. After four years of working together, this was the first time he had witnessed Stone stand up for his detectives.

An hour before they would typically call it a day, Dixie stood up, grabbed her keys and cell phone, and turned to Rock. "I'm going home. I want you to understand, I'm not mad at you, even though I desperately want to be. As I'm sure you could see, I'm not exactly shy but this... this is just too much. Knowing that someone was watching me, taking pictures, maybe even listening. It's just a lot to take in."

"I understand. I just want you to know I did what I thought was right. And it just about killed me to have to do things this way."

"I get it. I would have done the same if the roles were reversed. Right now, though. I just want to go home. By myself."

She pulled into her driveway, evening had just started to settle in. Through the window, under the shade of oak trees that lined the front of her house, she saw a light flicker off the living room wall. She hadn't turned the television on for days and she never left any lights on. She closed her car door as quietly as she could and ran to her house with her back to the siding, gun drawn. She crept along the bushes that adorned the house until she got to the picture window. Lined up with the window frame, heart pounding, she carefully turned her head to peer inside. Branden was sitting on her couch, socked feet propped on the coffee table, eating a bag of potato chips. "Son of a bitch," she cried before stomping through the bushes. She slammed the front door open, knowing he didn't lock it behind him. "Branden, what the hell? You scared the shit out of me. You do remember I carry a gun, right?" She set it on the small desk in front of the window and then thought better of. She picked it back up and put it in her waistband.

"Hey. I didn't expect you home so early." He sat up and pulled his feet off the table. "As much as I'd appreciate not being killed by my own sister, people trying to shoot me is par for the course."

Dixie shook her head. "Get over here."

Branden stood and wrapped his arms around her. The two weren't as close as Dixie wished they could be. Being able to hug him brought her a sense of serenity and it was the closest to home she ever felt.

She loosened her grip and backed away to arm's length. "Listen, I'm glad you stopped by and were able to get something to eat. I'm also pissed that you broke into my house. But it's not safe for you to be here right now."

Branden laughed. "Dixie, it's not safe for me to be anywhere, at any time. That's why I stopped by. I have to leave in the morning. I think I might be pushing my luck here right now."

She tilted her head and frowned. "I know that's true. But, seriously. I'm not even sure it's safe for me to be here now." She glanced at the floor and saw Branden's bags tucked against the edge of the couch. She sighed and shook her head. "You can't stay here tonight."

"I promise, I'll be gone before you get up in the morning. I won't even steal any money." His smile was hopeful and pleading.

"Jokes aside, you can't stay. I'm sorry, Branden"

"Fine. I'll leave now then. I'll call you in a few days to let you know I'm okay." He slipped his sneakers on and grabbed his bags. "Thanks for the hospitality." He slammed the door on his way out and Dixie watched him fade away through the picture window.

She sat on the couch and buried her face in her hands. For as long as she could remember, Branden had masked his hurt and sadness as anger. She didn't ever want to tell him "no" but given the current situation, it wasn't safe for either of them to be around the other. And she couldn't tell him that someone was watching her. Branden was the protective kind, even though he could barely manage to take care of himself. If he knew someone was watching her, he would have camped outside her house all night without thinking about the risk of drawing his enemies right to him, and ultimately, to her.

A few years ago, she had found herself in that exact position. She was held captive in Georgia by four men who were looking for Branden. The people that were following him were an untrusting sort and they refused to believe her when she told them she didn't know where he was. For three days, she was a prisoner in her own house. Fortunately, it was one of the rare occasions that Branden popped into town. On the third day, he dropped by her house to say hello and saw her, through the window, incapacitated. Catching a side view of one of her captor's faces, and recognizing him as one of the men looking for him, he left and made it to a safe distance before calling them and drawing them away from Dixie.

For weeks afterward, Dixie couldn't shake the idea that Branden was dead. When he was finally able to call her to let her know he was safe, he called expecting a thank you for saving her life. As relieved as Dixie was to know that he was safe and alive, she was also furious with him. She screamed at him over the phone and made it clear that the reason she was in that position to begin with was because of him. She refused to thank him and the two of them spend the next six months with no contact at all. Dixie knew he put his own life at risk by calling the men away from her but she wouldn't back down from where she stood on the matter. Once they started talking again, their relationship remained strained for two years. Every day, Dixie could feel it tearing her apart piece by piece. They didn't have much in common but they were the only family they had.

Before heading to bed that night, Dixie tried reversing the call from the last time Branden had called her.

"We're sorry. The number you've reached is no longer in service."

The next morning, Dixie walked in to the station with two cups of coffee and slid one onto Rock's desk as a sort of peace offering. He took it in his hands and looked up at her, concern buried deep in his eyes.

"Does this mean you're not mad anymore?"

"I was never mad. I told you that. It's just not something I'm typically willing to share or talk about openly with my partner or my boss, for that matter. I do my best to keep my private life private, you know?"

"I do. I completely understand. I try to do the same thing. Unfortunately, it doesn't always work."

"Agreed. Especially when your partner drives by your house and calls in to have patrol officers drive by all night long."

"Shit. You noticed that, huh?"

She raised her eyebrows. "I'm a detective. It's almost impossible not to notice." She sat down and booted up her computer and didn't say another word to him for the next hour.

"Excuse me." Morgan stepped around the police officer she had been speaking to when Rock and Dixie walked in. "You must be the detectives?" She offered them a wide smile and put her hand out to shake theirs.

"Uh, yeah. I'm Detective Rockefeller. This is Detective Lane. And you are?"

"I'm Morgan. Alexandria's mother. Officer Ruiz told me you'd be stopping by soon."

Morgan seemed to be the youngest of the mothers so far and she had the highest amount of energy. At first glance, it didn't look like she had been to sleep yet. Her hair was brushed and her makeup had been freshly applied. She was wearing a pair of jeans and a tank top. A gold necklace fell around her neck while multiple gold bracelets adorned her wrists. "You seem very composed."

"Only on the outside, Detective Lane. Inside, I feel like I've been shattered into a million pieces. But getting upset and acting crazy isn't going to help any of us. Trust me, as soon as the last person leaves, I'm going to completely lose it."

Dixie immediately came to the conclusion that she didn't trust Morgan. She had met a few people over the years who were able to maintain their composure during times of extreme stress but Morgan seemed to be trying a bit too hard. "We're going to go have a look around and then we'll sit down and get some information from you."

"Sounds great." Morgan was hot on their heels as the two of them made their way to the nursery.

Dixie and Rock both slowed and turned around. Morgan narrowly missed slamming into them. "We," Dixie motioned back and forth between herself and Rock, "are going to look around. We'll come back out here to speak to you."

"Oh." Morgan frowned and dropped her shoulders like she had never been told 'no' before. Fortunately, she listened and turned away from them.

Rock nudged Dixie with his elbow. "I'm going to let you interview this one."

"Ohh, no. I've had three already. This one is all yours." She walked into the nursery and turned back to look at Rock. "She's weird. It's almost like she's...excited that this is happening to her."

"I was thinking the same thing. Not only is she extremely composed, but she's eager to put herself in the spotlight. And, not to mention, trying to look good while doing so."

Dixie nodded and began looking around. The nursery didn't seem to match the rest of the apartment. The living room was full of matching pieces and they didn't look cheap. The nursery furniture was a mash up. Each piece was a different color and different material. The walls were a dingy beige and the carpet was a murky green and looked like it had seen its fair share of life. The colors were depressing at best and not at all fitting for a newborn. She busied herself looking through a stack of books on a small table that was hidden in the corner. This was the first time they had found more than one or two books but Dixie was sad to find that none of them contained any nursery rhymes.

Gemini walked in while Rock was crouched down, looking under the dresser.

"Hey. How are things looking so far?"

Rock shrugged and stood up. "Hey. Not great this time. I don't see anything. No clue, no ball, nothing. And I have to go interview our victim now."

Gemini shook her head. "Speaking of... did you two get accosted by her when you walked in also? She's a little too eager for my liking."

"I think that's the exact same word Rock used. And, yes, we did. She seemed happy to see us. Welcomed us like she was hosting a dinner party."

"That was my experience as well. Have fun with this one, Rock."

He tried to give her a look that said he was annoyed with her but knew failed miserably.

Gemini blew him a kiss before he walked out the door.

"Morgan? Let's have a seat at the table and we'll chat a bit."

"I'm okay standing. If someone else comes in..."

Rock didn't say a word but pulled out a chair and hung on to the back of it until she complied.

"Your daughter, Alexandria? Is her father still in the picture?"

Dixie looked at him out of the corner of her eye. She could tell just by the tone of his voice that he wasn't willing to entertain any games she might try to play with him.

"No. I don't actually know who he is. I went out one night and made a bad decision. But, I don't regret any of it because it gave me my daughter."

"Mhm." Rock jotted notes on his notepad while he continued talking. "Where'd you get all the furniture in the nursery? I can't help but notice everything out here matches but the nursery is full of random pieces that you just threw together."

She sighed. "I did. What you see out here was partially funded by my father. He bought it all and I paid him back for half of it over a few years. I don't have that much money and when I found out I was pregnant, I hate to admit this, but I bought all the furniture used. It was all clean and I figured it would be better to make sure she was clothed and fed rather than spending thousands of dollars that I don't have on a matching furniture set."

As much of an excuse as he thought it was, that explanation made perfect sense to Rock. He couldn't hold making a smart decision against her. "Walk me though what you did tonight starting with the time you put Alexandra to bed."

"It's Alexandria."

Rock purposely mispronounced her name to see if his feelings about Morgan were correct. She was either quicker than he thought she was or she was telling the truth.

"I read her a story, like I do every night. I watched television for about thirty minutes and scrolled mindlessly through social media. I poked my head in to make sure she was asleep and then I went in to take a shower. I went to bed."

"Did you notice anything out of the ordinary? A smell, a sound?"

"No, nothing. I follow the same routine every day."

"And when did you notice Alexandria was missing and what did you do when you found out?"

"I woke up and realized I hadn't heard her cry yet so I got up to check on her. When I went in to the nursery, she was gone. I called the police right away. When I got off the phone, I brushed my hair and put on some makeup so I didn't scare people away and then I opened my door and waited for people to show up."

Rock took a deep breath to keep himself from commenting on how self-absorbed she was. "Does anyone else have access to your apartment? A boyfriend, parent?"

She had to think about it for a minute. "Nope. Just me. I prefer privacy."

Like always, they didn't bother going home. They stopped to get a cup of coffee on their way in and proceeded to process whatever paperwork they could before heading out for the day. Rock's desk phone rang a few minutes after seven. It was Gemini.

"Can you put me on speaker? I'll fill Dixie in too."

Rock hit the speaker button and hung up the receiver.

"Thanks. Hi, Dixie. I'm calling you on this phone so I can talk to both of you at once. I know none of us were feeling great about Morgan while we were there last night and I think I know why. Or, at least, kind of know why. While my team was there we didn't find any clues like the previous scenes. We also didn't find a ball. What we did find, under the edge of that nauseating salmon throw rug, was an indentation in the carpet. It didn't look like it was more than a few days old. Usually, in an apartment, they use pretty cheap carpeting because they have to replace it all the time. The cheap carpets hold the indentation for a few days to a week or until you vacuum it. We moved the rug and found the other three marks in the carpet."

"So, maybe she moved around the nursery."

"She didn't. None of the furniture in that room matched the measurements we took from the carpet. The desk that was in her living room, however, matched perfectly."

"Is it a heavy one? Maybe she just found someone who would be able to help her move it out of the room?"

"It's possible. But it's not just that. Not only was that desk in the nursery within the last few days, but we don't have any clues, and this was only the third day."

"What do you mean?"

"I mean, every other call has been four days from the last. This one was only three days. I don't know if I'm right but I do know you should probably check into it further. She seemed way too eager to help. I'm just not quite sure why."

Rock ended the call and stared at Dixie. "I'm too tired for this. Was she saying she doesn't think Morgan's daughter is missing?"

"It sounded to me like she doesn't think Morgan *has* a daughter."

Their first stop was to visit Morgan again. Rock pounded on her door, not allowing any chance for her to say she didn't hear it. When she opened it, he didn't wait for an invitation. He walked in and went directly toward the nursery to see the marks that Gemini had told them about. Dixie spoke to Morgan hoping to either catch her in a lie or get some valuable information. She asked for Alexandria's birth date, where she was born, who came to see her when she was in the hospital. They were all basic questions but could easily stump someone who wasn't telling the truth. Morgan held her own and was able to answer each question as it came. Dixie continued her strategy and kept firing questions at her until Rock came out and said he was ready to go.

They drove straight to the hospital Morgan named as the one she gave birth to Alexandria in. The sterile smell of hospitals always made Dixie anxious. It wasn't the idea of it being clean, rather she associated the smell with sickness and death. She had felt that way for as far back as she could remember and she didn't know why. She also hated how cold they were. As soon as they walked through the doors she could feel the cold clawing at her skin. She rubbed the backs of her arms with her hands as they made their way to the nurses' station. Dixie was hoping they would be able to bring up the birth information with no problems so they could move forward with their investigation. Rock, being the more skeptical of the two, hoped they were able to prove the baby wasn't born there.

They both flashed their badges and Rock took the lead. The nurse was an older woman with curly gray hair and big glasses. Her name badge read "Marianne- Head Nurse". She was heavy set but carried her size well. "Good morning, Marianne." When she opened her mouth to speak, seeing the look on her face, Rock cut her off. "I know all about patient confidentiality but I'm not asking for any of that. All I need to know is if a particular baby was born at this hospital. I don't need anything printed, I don't need any information other than a simple yes or no."

"Now, Detective, you know I can't give you anything without a warrant."

"Just a verbal yes or no and we'll be on our way."

The nurse harrumphed but sat down and moved the mouse to wake up her computer screen without saying a word.

Rock, assuming she would give them exactly what he had asked and nothing more, spoke again. "The mother's name is Morgan Miller. She says she gave birth on January twenty-eighth. A baby girl named Alexandria Miller."

Marianne clicked and typed and clicked some more. She looked up at Rock and shook her head. "Nothing."

"Can you expand the search? Look for the last name sometime within the month?"

"I already did. I looked up both Morgan and Miller for January and February and I don't have anything. Are you sure you have the right hospital?"

"Yup. Just not sure we have the right person. Thank you for your time and cooperation."

Marianne nodded in acknowledgment.

"So, what do we do now?" Dixie couldn't tell if he was relieved or angry.

"We go back to Morgan's... again."

As they rounded the corner into her hallway, they nearly bumped in to her.

She jumped back, startled. "Detectives. You're here again."

"And we almost missed you. Where are you headed all dressed up?'

Morgan had on fresh makeup and was wearing a pair of black leggings with a cream colored, thigh length t-shirt. Brown ankle boots were at her feet, a gold chain wrapped around her waist. Her gold jewelry from the night before was still present. "I'm... ahh. I'm just going out, to meet a friend. She thought I could use some cheering up."

"Well, you should probably call her and tell her you're going to be a little late." Dixie put her hand on the back of Morgan's arm and turned her back toward her apartment. "You know, Morgan, you look awfully put together for someone who was "going to lose it" as soon as we all left last night."

"Oh. You should have seen me once everyone left. I was a mess."

"I'm sure. Except, you looked just like this when we saw you earlier. Of course, you've changed your clothes and put fresh makeup on."

"I had to use a lot. You know, to cover up the puffiness and all."

Rock pointed toward the nursery and they followed him in. "So? Why did you move your desk?"

"I'm sorry?"

"Your desk, the one that was right here just a few days ago. The one that's currently in your living room."

Morgan opened her mouth but didn't speak right away. "I, um, it was in the way. It worked when I used this as a spare room but with Alexandria, it didn't make sense anymore."

"And Alexandria, you said she was born at St. Mary's, right?"

"Yeah. On January twenty-eighth. No, excuse me, she was born at Northwestern. Why are you asking me all these questions?"

"Because we don't think you're telling us the truth. See, we went to Northwestern this morning and they have no record of you giving birth there. Can you explain that?"

"They must be mistaken. That's all."

"Mhm. Can you show us the paperwork from when you were discharged?"

"Sure, yeah. I can find it for you. I'll bring it by the station tomorrow."

Dixie smiled and tilted her head. "I think he meant now."

"Oh." Morgan put her head down and left the nursery, scuffing her feet along the carpet.

Dixie and Rock could hear her opening and closing drawers and shuffling papers. About five minutes later she returned to the nursery empty handed.

"I'm sorry. I can't seem to find it. I've been so tired since she was born, I'm lucky I can remember my own name. I'm sure I'll come across it."

"I somehow doubt that." Rock mumbled. "Can we see a picture of her?"

"Yeah, sure." Morgan took her phone out of her pocket and hit a few buttons before turning the phone towards them. She smiled. "Here she is."

"Do you have a better one? Maybe one of the two of you or those cute monthly ones that everyone seems to be doing now?" They both stood still while she fumbled through her phone, frantically looking for a picture that she knew wasn't in there. Dixie put her hand over the top of Morgan's phone to stop her search. "Okay, seriously, Morgan. In that amount of time, I could have showed off eighty-five pictures of my cat and you couldn't come up with a second one of your own child? We're going to go in the kitchen and sit at the table. You're going to stop playing games and you're going to tell us the truth about what you're really doing."

Forty-five minutes later, they had almost a full statement from her. "She told me I wouldn't get caught. She promised me that it was harmless. It was just supposed to get your attention. You weren't supposed to find out." Now, for the first time, Morgan was showing emotion. She was scared, and angry, and on the verge of tears.

"Who is 'she'?"

"Nina. She's a community activist and she's also a close friend."

"Nina Carrera? That psychopath who believes citizens should be in charge and police shouldn't have jobs?"

"Yes, that Nina. But she's not a psychopath. She's really smart and if people would just listen to her..."

"I'm never going to listen to her. And right now, I'm done listening to you. Can you stand up please?"

Morgan did as requested.

"Morgan Miller, you are under arrest for reporting a false crime to the police. You have the right to remain silent," he clicked the second cuff into place. "Anything you say, can and will be used against you in a court of law."

After filling Stone in on their morning and afternoon, Dixie finally got a chance to inquire about who Nina was.

"Nina Carrera: concerned citizen, self-proclaimed activist, feminist. You have a rally or a protest of any sort and she's right there on the front line. She's the one who carries a bullhorn and will argue against anything you say. She has a pretty good following because, lucky for her, people are stupid. Groupies, I believe they're called, who will believe anything she says simply because she says it. She could hold a duckling in her hand and show it to them all. She'd swear it was blue and they would all claim they saw a blue duck as well."

"That's pretty terrifying, actually. I mean, I know there are people like that out there, but knowing she has an entire following."

"And it's worse for us because she believes the police are useless. I'm kind of surprised she hasn't formed a watch group for this case yet."

"A watch group?"

"Yup. She has taken to sending her fellow concerned citizens out to follow us when she doesn't feel we're doing a good enough job to solve a case. Refuses, of course, to take responsibility for hindering our ongoing investigations. She's been arrested numerous times for it."

"Ooh, I can't wait to meet her. She sounds almost as fun as Leila." Dixie bounced her eyebrows up and down.

"She's so much worse." Rock pointed at her, "and don't ever do that eyebrow thing again.

Anyway, lucky for you, you get to meet her soon. Let's go."

After speaking with a neighbor, they found Nina at a small park on the south side of the city. She had short, curly black hair and wore gold hoop earrings. She had on a striped t-shirt and a pair of taper legged jeans. As rock had mentioned, her mouth was covered by a bullhorn and Dixie couldn't make out a word she was saying. Rock walked up behind her. "Nina Carrera. We need just a moment of your time."

She turned her head just enough to see who was calling her name. "I have every right to be here, detective. You know that."

Rock ripped the bullhorn from her hands when she tried to shout through it again. "We need a minute of your time. Now."

"Oh, well, why didn't you say so? It's about time you came to me for advice. You know I always believed you were smarter than you pretended to be but I'm surprised it's taken you this long to seek me out for a good reason."

He pulled a pair of handcuffs from his waistband for the second time that day. "Nina Carrera, You are under arrest for conspiracy."

"Conspiracy? For what?"

"You have the right to remain silent."

They were both mentally exhausted. Between conducting interviews and heading interrogations, neither of them thought they could handle any more. The conspiracy theories and utter nonsense that came from both Morgan and Nina were enough to make any person of average intelligence insane. Dixie and Rock both went straight home after work, neither having the energy to even sit in a bar somewhere.

Dixie laid in her bed, staring at the ceiling, dreading the inevitable phone call. She had even changed her clothes so she wouldn't have to worry about it and could just leave when the time came.

The call came in right on cue.

Jacqueline looked exhausted. Her appearance and reaction to what was happening was what they had expected to see in every other mother so far. Overwhelmed with worry, upset, and fighting a stage of shock. They could tell she had been crying, her makeup was smeared below her lashes and washed away on her cheeks. Her eyes were puffy and red, but she had managed to gain back some of her composure, enough so that she could speak to the police and tell them what had happened. She was wearing a pair of yoga pants and a tank top and Dixie couldn't help but wonder if it was an outfit or what she wore to bed, although her hair told them she was obviously asleep. At least she hadn't taken the time to make sure she looked perfect.

So far, this was the nicest nursery they had seen and the most inviting. The walls were painted a soft gray and offset by eggshell white furniture. There was a collection of pink and gray elephants of all kinds spread throughout the room. On the far wall behind the crib was a pink, white, and dark gray decal tree. The room was comfortable and calming.

The bottom drawer of the changing table was pulled open about two inches and Dixie knelt down in front of it. Without touching it, she tried her best to see what was inside. "Hey, Rock." She gestured for him to join her.

He knelt down beside her and turned on his phone screen so they could see better inside the drawer. "Is that a knife?" He used his gloved hands to pull it opened wider. Laying on top of a stack of diapers was a butcher's knife with three pair of sunglasses closed around the blade.

Gemini walked in and leaned down to look over their shoulders. "Ah. Three blind mice. Is that the new nursery rhyme or a stab at us? No pun intended."

"Could be both at this point." He stood up, careful not to back into her. "We didn't find the ball yet."

"Jacqueline. Can you tell us what happened after you put Savannah to bed?"

The following twenty minutes went the same it always did.

"And is her father still a part of her life?"

"I hate to admit it but I don't know who he is. I broke up with my boyfriend and about two weeks later, a couple of friends wanted to take me out. I went out three days that week and well...I didn't come home alone. I've never done that before. I guess I just wanted to not feel so alone."

"Do you know who any of the men are?"

She hung her head and her hair fell in her face. "No. I didn't bother to ask for any of their numbers. I wasn't looking for a relationship, just... I'm still so upset with myself for doing that. It's not who I am."

"You don't need to explain yourself or justify your actions. You're an adult, you can make your own decisions."

"I know but I just keep thinking about how I'm supposed to explain that to Savannah when she asks me where her dad is." Tears sprang to her eyes. "Now, I don't know if I'll ever even have the chance to explain it." She pressed her hands to her face and sobbed.

"You will. We're going to find her for you."

Rock had just sat at his desk when his phone chimed. It was a text from Gemini, the bingo ball was I-eighteen. She had found it tucked in the turned-up trunk of one of the larger stuffed elephants.

"Is there any significance to where we're finding the balls? I feel like some are being left in the open and others are hidden or simply tossed in the nursery as an afterthought. I mean, we've found what, two of them, on the floor?"

Rock nodded. "I suppose they could have fallen from where they were originally left. But, let's take a look anyway. And we'll get the numbers up while we're at it." He pulled the white board closer to their desks and started a new list marking where the balls were found. On the map, he placed a sticker with the number of each ball on it and added the new residence. He took a step back and examined the new pieces. "This tells me nothing."

"What else have we found since we last added to it? Calls are four days apart. We still have different stories for the fathers, the personalities are all still different taking the new case into consideration."

"Let's look at what is similar and why that would be important. Maybe it'll give us an idea of what to look for in the perp. We'll start with the fact that they're all single."

"It makes them easy targets. It would be harder to pull off if there was more than one adult in the house."

"Okay," Rock wrote in a small unused corner of the board. "What else?"

Dixie had to think for a minute. "Maybe he's not good with women. He gets turned down a lot. Maybe he sees single mothers as sluts and is blaming them for something?"

"I can see that."

"Daddy issues. He could have grown up in a household with no father, probably one without a lot of money. Maybe he's resentful of that."

"That also makes sense. But seems to me, he would be taking males if that was the case."

"Or maybe you're not looking for a man."

Rock and Dixie, both startled, looked toward the hallway. "Henry. When did you get here?"

"A few minutes ago. Stone called me yesterday." He extended his hand and Dixie took it. "Henry Mackaby, profiler."

"Nice to meet you. I'm Dixie." She smiled and released his hand.

Rock cleared his throat. "You really think a woman could be responsible for this?"

"Very much so. Men would most likely go after children but not infants. Most males who take children do so for reasons of a sexual nature. An infant wouldn't qualify. When someone takes a baby, it's because of a personal feeling. An instinct, most likely maternal. I believe you're looking for a woman in her thirties or forties. Probably single, with no children. She may have trouble getting pregnant. Without having many details of the case, I'm going to guess that the women who have become victims to the kidnapper are seen as, not the most motherly types. Your kidnapper is probably going on the basis that if she can't have a child, women who don't appreciate their children shouldn't have one either."

"Do you think they're still alive?" They could hear the concern in Rock's voice when he asked the question.

"I do. I'm not quite sure how one would keep that many infants a secret from neighbors or friends, but I don't believe they're dead. I think if that was the purpose, the kidnapper would kill the mother and leave the baby unharmed."

"And what about the nursery rhymes, the bingo balls, the fact that a new infant is disappearing every four days?"

"I don't have that many details yet. Let me take a look at your case notes and I'll get back to you."

Stone scheduled a second press conference now that Nina had inserted herself into their investigations one again. It wasn't a long conference but he was pissed and neither of his detectives blamed him, aside from the fact that he had been hands off since the beginning. Nina and Morgan had both made bail the day before on a promise to appear in court. They would likely get community service but it was still better than nothing. Toward the end of the conference, Dixie nudged Rock with her elbow and jerked her head to his right. He looked over and saw Leila Romero and Nina Carrera deep in conversation. There was nothing he could do until the taping part was complete but he kept his eye on the two of them for the entire round of questions.

As was his luck, as soon as Stone called the end, Nina and Leila separated. "Leila!" Rock shouted from his place on the risers.

She rolled her eyes up toward him. "What do you want? I'm busy, Detective."

Dixie touched his arm to tell him she was going to stay back with Stone.

He hurried toward Leila before she could walk away. "As much as I would love to see you behind bars, I hope Nina told you she got arrested yesterday. I'd watch your step when talking to her."

"Nina gave me a lot of really great information. The difference between us though, is I go through the appropriate channels to get what I need. I'm not looking to cause any trouble for myself or anyone else. And I know you hate that I'm good at what I do, Detective Rockefeller, that's why I'll never give you the satisfaction of arresting me."

"I hope for your sake you can trust her."

"Oh, I don't need to trust her. The more stupid things she does, the better my stories are. All I need to do is not piss her off."

Rock began to walk away before he was called back.

"Hey, Rockefeller."

He turned to see Leila digging in her leather bag. "Tell you friend over there that I keep my promises." She tossed what she was holding to him and walked away.

Rock put his hand out to catch it and turned it over in his palm. A dog bone. He put it in his pocket and forget about it until his phone rang a few hours later. He took it out and set it on his desk.

Dixie curled up her lip. "Are you that hungry or are you now keeping evidence as souvenirs?"

Rock hesitated a moment trying to figure out what she was talking about and then it hit him. "I forgot about the dog bones." He picked it up and practically sprinted to the white board. He held it up next to the picture with the bones in the shoe. "It's the same kind. Common, but the same." He started pacing back and forth, tapping the bone on his thigh.

Dixie's eyes followed him back and forth. "Would you care to fill me in?"

He tossed the bone on her desk. "This one is for you. It's from Leila." He continued pacing.

Dixie laughed loudly. "Wow. She really shouldn't have. As pissed as I should be, that's actually really funny. I'll give her credit for that. But why are you...oh! You're not thinking it's Leila, are you?"

"She is a woman. She doesn't have any children. The first article she wrote didn't exactly show quality women from her perspective. Isn't that exactly what Henry described when he was here this morning?"

"Almost exactly. Do you want to go talk to her now or wait until morning?"

"She was talking to Nina earlier and said she got some information from her. You and I both know Nina doesn't actually know anything. Let's wait until morning to see what comes out in that article of hers."

They walked out the front door of the station, ready to go home for the evening, but were greeted by a large gathering of Nina's followers standing across the street. As always, Nina was shouting nonsense through the bullhorn and her people were clapping and cheering and hollering back. They were all carrying various signs containing sayings like: BRING THE BABIES HOME. TRUST THE MOTHERS. One even had a sign covered in glitter calling for the removal of Larry Rockefeller and Dixie Land.

Rock's pace quickened and Dixie, as usual, was having a hard time keeping up with him. When she saw the glittered sign, she put her arm out and touched his shoulder. He turned to see her doubled over in laughter. "I'm sorry." She took a few deep breaths and tried her best to speak through her hysterics. "Now, I've seen it all. Do you see that glitter sign? Dixie Land!" She let out another guffaw, tears emerging from her eyes. "Nina is really smart. If people would just listen to her." She exploded into laughter again and Rock couldn't help but join in. "Clearly, her supporters aren't smart."

He was still mad about the rally but seeing Dixie get so much joy out of that sign almost made it worth it. By the time Dixie had pulled herself together, almost all the rally participants had turned in their direction. They were all still cheering and chanting but their eyes had focused on the two detectives. As they neared, Rock knew Nina was expecting them to approach her directly, so he walked straight past her. She was in the middle of spouting something through the bullhorn and she stuttered, losing her train of thought, when he didn't stop to talk to her. He had to force back the smile that was threatening to emerge on his face.

He approached the woman holding the glittered sign and smiled at her. "You know, your argument would have much more validity if you were able to get the names right?"

She looked confused and turned the sign to face her. "What's wrong with my sign? It's not my fault if you don't like being called out."

Rock wanted to laugh but controlled it. "It's your right. You have free speech. And you're more than welcome to make yourself look stupid whenever you want." He turned his shoulder toward Dixie. "Have you met my partner yet? This is Detective Lane?" He slowed down the pronunciation of her last name hoping it would click in her mind. When he didn't see it register he turned her sign toward her again and pointed to the sparkling word 'land'. "Lane. With an 'E'."

He walked away without looking back at her and strolled directly past Nina again to get to his car.

"You're not going to say anything to Nina?"

"I was going to. But hearing how disappointed she was when I didn't was all I needed. Let her cry about something she knows nothing about. She'll be back in jail sooner than later." He closed his door and started his car, leaving Dixie standing in the parking lot.

Rock knew he should have gone straight home. He was still angry about Nina and confused about the possibility of Leila being their perp. He wanted to read the article she was writing immediately. He didn't have the patience to wait for it to come out in print. If she really felt she had such great information, she would wait to post the electronic version until the morning when the ratings were higher. He pulled his car over to the side, thankful for a spot less than half a block down from the bar. He promised himself one drink and then he would go home even if Dixie or Gemini showed up. Knowing he'd be less comfortable and more likely to leave as he told himself he would, Rock sat on a stool at the bar and ordered a whiskey. The bartender, Tina, set it in front of him and placed her elbow on the bar.

"Must have been a long day. I don't think I've ever seen you sit here and I've known you for years."

"You could say that. Just a lot going on. But, I'm only having this one drink and then I'm going home."

She nodded and Rock watched her walk to the other end of the bar to speak to another gentleman sitting by himself. Tina was cute but not really his type. She was tall and had shoulder length blond hair. Her eyes were a pale blue but she always tried to darken them with black eyeliner. Rock guessed she was single, probably a little lonely. He could tell by the tone of her voice. She was always looking for conversation as brief as it may be and he thought maybe being at work was the only real human interaction she got. By the time his drink was two sips from being gone, he had convinced himself that she had five infants locked in her apartment somewhere, eagerly waiting for her to get home so they would be fed. He shook his head and put his face in his hands, rubbing his eyes, trying in a fruitless effort to get that image out of his head. He downed the last of his drink and dropped a ten dollar bill on the bar. He couldn't let this case get to him. Henry threw him completely off track when he said he believed they were looking for a woman and now Rock wanted to blame every female he saw.

As he approached his car he saw a sheet of paper under his wiper, flapping in the breeze. He cursed under his breath believing it was an advertisement of some sort. Without looking, he ripped it out of the windshield wiper and threw it on his passenger seat before getting in his car. It wasn't until he started the car that he saw the other items. He pulled on a pair of gloves and opened his door enough so he could wrap his arm around the front and grab the pieces of paper. Without looking at them, he picked up the paper from his passenger seat.

I can see more than you think I can,
Let's play a game.

He turned the small pages over in his hand. He had two photographs. The first was of his wife, pushing a baby carriage around the park. He knew it was the park closest to their home because he could see the apple tree in the background. It always seemed out of place to him and he believed it was the only one in the city. The second photo was a close-up of his daughter, Ella. It was so close, he could see only her face and part of her torso. The image had clearly been cropped and Rock couldn't make out anything that was in the background. The photo could have been taken anywhere.

He slammed his car into drive and squealed his tires pulling onto the road. He needed to make sure his wife and baby were safe.

Chapter VI

They'd have to pay attention to this one. He was around too often and they couldn't risk him getting in their way.

He didn't take the time to call Gemini or Stone. He concentrated on weaving in and out of evening traffic trying to make it home as quickly as he could, safely. He cursed at himself for not turning on the dashboard camera like Stone had asked him to do, even when he wasn't home. He didn't like the idea of his privacy being invaded but now that he had a picture of his wife and daughter and it was clear that whoever it was knew he was at the bar, he understood how Dixie had felt a week prior when the same thing had happened to her. He no longer cared about his privacy, he cared about the safety and well-being of his family.

He pulled into his driveway, which he never does, and flung the front door of his house open. "Jill," he called her name so loud it echoed through the house. His heart was pounding, he didn't think he had ever been so scared in his life. He poked his head into the kitchen and, not seeing anyone, turned to check the bedrooms. He called his wife's name again and he could feel his mind racing with all the different scenarios that he may be facing when he found them. He checked the nursery, their bedroom, and both bathrooms. Making his way to the kitchen again, he yelled his wife's name for the third time. All the muscles in his body weakened when he saw her coming through the sliding glass door that led from the kitchen to the deck out back. He didn't speak and didn't give her the chance to. He immediately wrapped his arms around her and pulled her close, leaning forward to kiss Ella on the top of her head.

"I don't think I've ever been so happy to see you two."

Rock spent nearly two hours explaining to his wife why he was so worried when he got home. He made her go through everything she had done for the past three days and tried to get her to remember anything that may have been out of the ordinary, even if it didn't seem so at the time. At times, he felt as though he was coaching her, which is one thing he prided himself on having never done while interrogating suspects. There were many other ways to get the information needed without trying to plant ideas in their head. With his wife, he couldn't help it. He couldn't seem to get her to understand why every little detail she could remember may be helpful.

Jill was getting frustrated with him for asking so many questions and having her repeat what she had already told him four times over. He was getting frustrated with her because she wasn't giving him the details he was asking for. The intelligent part of him knew she couldn't give details she didn't have, but the protective part of him needed her to give more than she had been. The conversation had been unsuccessful for both parties and they eventually gave up. Rock put Ella to bed, showered, and curled up with his wife in their bed.

Dixie woke up early the next morning and grabbed her phone to check for Leila's article. She found it easily but was let down by how short it was. She read through all four paragraphs and found herself disappointed by every word of it. There was nothing in it that they could use against her. For the second time, she didn't give any actual information. The majority of it was quotes from Nina about how she felt the police weren't doing anything. One entire paragraph focused on how they had spent an entire day investigating a kidnapping case that didn't fit with the current ones at all. Dixie was livid about Nina trying to use what she had concocted herself, against them. And, as she suspected, not a single word was mentioned attesting to that fact.

She knew it was early but she chanced calling Rock's cell phone anyway.

"Rockefeller."

"Sorry to call so early. I wanted to save you the anger that might come from reading..."

"You're about five minutes too late. If murder wasn't illegal..."

"That's about how I'm feeling at the moment. Who do they think they are trying to use that against us? We spent all day investigating a case that they made up, for the exact purpose of making us investigate it. Anyway, like I said, I was just hoping to save you the aggravation. I'm going to shower and eat and then I'll be heading in. You want coffee?"

"I'll be heading in shortly myself. I have to stop at the lab first. I'll grab the coffee on my way."

They both hung up and Rock grumbled under his breath, fighting the urge to let an ear shattering growl escape his lips.

He had texted Gemini late the night before asking her to meet him at the lab early. He walked in immediately after her and caught her before she entered the secure area. He handed her the photos and the note and explained to her that he had grabbed the note without thinking about it. He didn't want her to get too excited when she pulled a print because he was ninety-nine percent certain it would be his. She thanked him for the warning and told him she would call him soon.

"Oh! Before you leave? The sunglasses from yesterday. I tested all of them on the off chance that someone had put them on their face." She watched Rocks eyes widen. "They didn't. But there was one pair that had a tiny smudge on the lens. I tried to pull a print and failed and no DNA was present. I know it's not great news but it is possible that your perp might be getting a little careless. Take some extra precautions and make sure the uniforms don't destroy your scenes. We may have a break coming up soon."

Rock thanked her and left. He stopped for coffee, as he promised, and got to the station shortly after Dixie.

"Thank you." She took the cup from him and sipped it slowly so she didn't burn her mouth. "So, what's the plan for today? Do you still want to go talk to Leila?"

"I sure do. Let's just make sure Stone hasn't gotten to her first because I'm pretty sure I could hear him yelling this morning from across town."

"Ohh. I didn't even think about that. He's going to be pissed."

"With good reason, just like the two of us. Has Henry stopped by yet today? I was hoping to hear from him by now."

Right on cue he walked through the door. "Good morning."

Rock and Dixie murmured their greetings.

Henry sat on top of the empty desk that was across from them. "I had a chance to look at the files yesterday. This is a tough one. Your kidnapper is leaving you with almost nothing to work with."

"Tell me about it." Rock was annoyed by hearing that statement out loud.

"You asked me to look for significance of the four day span and I did, but I couldn't come up with any one thing that would make sense. I could hypothesize all day long but that wouldn't do much good. It's possible it's something as simple as a work schedule they're following. I'm still sticking with my original thought that you are looking for a woman rather than a man. The nursery rhymes, I'm at a loss. It would make sense if they were somehow connected to the decor in the rooms or if they were following a numeric pattern, but they're not. They seem as random as everything else."

"What about the bingo balls? Do you have any insight for those?"

"Nothing. I mean, there is a nursery rhyme titled "Bingo" but other than that, unless you've missed a bingo card somewhere, I don't have any answers. The only thing I can tell you is maybe this is their way of playing games." Henry took his leave shortly after.

"Great. So even our profiler can't give us any more insight than what we had yesterday."

Although Dixie could understand his frustration he still seemed a little tenser than he should be. "Are you okay today? You seem to be a bit on edge."

Rock shook his head. "My stalker came back. They followed me to the bar when I left here last night and left a picture of my wife and my baby on my windshield."

Dixie saw the look of hurt and worry in his eyes. "They followed you? Did you get a look at them?"

Rock shook his head again. "I didn't know until I came out of the bar about twenty minutes later. They must have followed me straight from work."

"Does your wife know?" Dixie had concern in her voice. Even though she hadn't yet met his wife or his daughter, when you work as a detective, your partner's family becomes your family as well. Partners look out for each other both at work and at home.

"I told her. She's scared, of course. She begged me last night not to come to work today and cried herself to sleep. I don't think she's worried about me or even about herself, she's worried about Ella. I can only assume she won't let her out of her sight at all today. She'll be bringing her in the bathroom with her so she can keep that close of an eye on her."

Stone came in and went straight to their desks instead of his office for probably the first time ever. "I assume you read Leila's article?" He leaned against the empty desk with his hands crossed in front of him.

"We did. We were waiting on you to see if you had laid into her yet or not."

"You know, I was going to but I stopped by the lab first to speak to Gemini. Seems you got there before I did." He gave Rock an accusatory look. "I'm not sure what I need to do or say to get you to understand that I need to know when these things are happening. What do you not get about this?"

Rock gave him a moment to make sure he wasn't going to be interrupted. "I understand that you need to know. I was going to tell you when you got here. Last night, when I received the note and pictures, I wasn't at home. My top priority was getting home to make sure my wife and daughter were safe, just as any other detective, including yourself, would have done. Now I have to assume, since this person followed me to where I was, they couldn't possibly be stupid enough to follow me home as well."

"You don't get to make that decision." Stone was angry and his voice echoed in the nearly empty room. "The correct course of action would have been to call it in so we could have had a patrol car swing by your house. Then you call me. Then you go home."

"Patrol? So they could go inform my wife that she might be in danger? No, thank you. Besides, I wasn't that far from home. I probably would have been the first one there anyway." He looked at his desk and shook his head knowing he should have followed protocol but was too stubborn to back down now. "I would appreciate it if we could call in a favor and have someone do a few rounds by the house throughout the day. Jill is scared and I think it would make her feel better to see a few cars go by so she knows she's being looked out for." It was so hard for him to admit that. Rock hated asking for help no matter how much he needed it.

Stone stood up. "I'll make a few phone calls. You two go talk to Leila and get Gemini's team back out the scenes. Have them check everywhere, under the cribs, on the back and sides of dressers to see if they can find a bingo card." Rock and Dixie both cocked their heads. "I ran into Henry on my way in." He closed himself in his office and picked up his phone.

Rock had no intention of extending the same courtesy he did the week before. He was planning on waltzing into the news station and demanding to speak to Leila. Fortunately, like the last time, just as they were approaching the door, she was coming out.

She stopped and did a half turn, contemplating walking back inside. She hung her head instead. "Oh, Christ. What do you want now? I didn't give away any of your precious information." Under her breath she added, "Not that you have any anyway."

"Where were you two nights ago?"

Leila let out a nervous laugh. "What?"

Rock would come back to the article later. He was hoping to catch her off guard with the questioning. "Two night ago. Where were you?"

"You've gotta be kidding me. I was at home. Depending on what time you're asking about, I was either making dinner, writing, or sleeping. I know you're not trying to blame me just because you're pissed off about my articles. So, what are you trying to get at?" Her hair was blowing in her face and she was struggling to speak in an authoritative tone around it. Even her body language had changed.

"It's just one of those things where you've given us a few details that aren't known to the public. So, we need to ask to determine whether it's coincidence or if there's a reason these things are coming from you."

"I would love to believe that, Rockefeller, but you can't possibly expect me to take you seriously after that mishap you had the other day. Investigating a case that wasn't even part of the current one. You two must have felt so stupid."

"For doing our job? No. We investigate everything that comes our way. Just because it doesn't fit with the current case doesn't mean it's not legit. However, did your friend Nina happen to let you in on the little tidbit that she was arrested for exactly that? She convinced one of her little followers to make up a kidnapping to get us to go out to her apartment. The case didn't fit because it was complete bullshit. The two of them wasted our entire day following leads that got us nowhere and interrupted our chances of finding something that could help us solve the real case. Those babies could be dead because of the stunt they pulled. And all of that nonsense you put in your article was exactly that, nonsense. The entire thing was based on lies because you believe and trust a woman who thinks the entire world is out to get her."

"It doesn't change the fact that you wasted your time knowing the case was different. I have to make decisions every day based on what is priority and the two of you clearly missed the mark on that. You can't blame your poor judgment on other people. Now, if you don't mind, I have a job to do. And I might suggest you try a little harder to do yours instead of bothering me all day. Find someone else who has time to waste." She walked away with her heels clicking on the cement sidewalk.

Rock decided it would be better to stop by the lab rather than calling Gemini. It was on their way back to the station anyway.

"Two visits in one day? This can't be good."

"Special request from Stone." Rock filled her in on what Henry had told them and asked, on Stone's behalf, for her to send her team back out in search of the bingo card.

"I can send a team out. But it's going to take us a few days to hit all five places again. Do you have a particular location that's priority or just hit them all until we hopefully find it?"

"I would start at the beginning. Henry didn't say but I'm guessing the first place would be where it was most likely hidden. If there is one hidden at all."

"All right. I'll get a team out after lunch."

"I appreciate it." They turned to leave and Gemini called out.

"Dixie? Can I talk to you for a minute?" She motioned to Rock to give them a minute.

"Are you okay? You seem to be focused on everything except what's going on today."

"Shit. I thought I was doing pretty good hiding it."

"Honey, you haven't said a word since you stepped through the door. You weren't looking at me, you weren't looking at Rock. Half the time you had your back turned to us. Is the case starting to get to you?"

Dixie sighed and closed her eyes briefly. "No. Not directly, anyway. It's just... I think... Hmm. I'm late and I'm really worried that I might be pregnant. I can't even bring myself to take a test because of this case. It would be bad enough regardless but all the baby talk and nurseries and infants missing... I just don't think I could handle it depending on the outcome."

"I see. And I understand. Would it be safe to assume it would be your *friends*?" She curled up her mouth at how the words came out. She wasn't sure what to call the man that Dixie was seeing.

Dixie scrunched up her face not wanting to tell the truth but knowing she had to. "I have more than one."

Gemini nodded her head and Dixie could tell she didn't hold any judgment. She appreciated that. "Well, you have my number. You can use it any time. And if you need someone to be there if you do decide to take a test." She let her sentence hang in the air and watched Dixie nod once in appreciation.

Dixie met Rock outside and walked straight past him on the way to the car. "Let's go."

Rock looked at her face when he slid onto the driver's seat and decided not to involve himself. Sometimes he was better off not knowing and he felt like this was probably one of those times.

The following two days were empty. They didn't get any new leads, there were no rallies, no new articles about the case. Dixie and Rock were beginning to get restless and their conversations were going in circles. Gemini called them towards the end of the second day to let them know that her team retraced all five apartments and didn't find a bingo card anywhere. It was disappointing but they were both glad her team hadn't just missed it the first time around.

Rock went straight home to spend the evening with his daughter and wife. He put Ella to bed and told his Jill he would be heading to bed in just a few minutes and pushed her to go in without him. Not wanting to put any unnecessary stress on her, he waited until he was sure she was laying down before taking the extra camera he had borrowed from work out of his pocket. He positioned it in the picture window in their living room, facing the driveway and his car. He didn't hold out much hope that he would be able to see anything definitive, but he was hoping whoever it was that was watching him, might not be able to see it nestled among the various plants that took up residence in that same window. If he could get something on camera, he would also be able to show Stone that he was listening to him, even though he always seemed to push back.

Rock checked the camera's live feed on his phone before showering and crawling in to bed. Jill was already fast asleep so he wrapped himself around her and fell asleep listening to the rhythm of her breathing.

Dixie was still half asleep by the time she got to the apartment. Rock didn't look like he was feeling much better. "You ready to do this again?"

Rock just shook his head and walked in. This nursery also was pink, although it was much more subdued than the last one with the frills. The color was offset by the white, wooden furniture. The window had sheer curtains and a baby pink valance on the top. There were decorative boxes alternating between pink and white. Baby bunny decals graced the tops of the walls and three stuffed bunnies were tucked in the corner of the crib.

Dixie knelt on the carpet to look under the bassinet that rested near the far wall next to the dresser. She backed up to a squatted position and looked at her pant leg. Hanging just off the edge of the dresser, so she couldn't see it when she was standing up, was a teapot, strung up by its handle so the spout was pointing down. "I guess we found our next clue. Tip me over and pout me out." She pointed to the dresser to show Rock and then to her knee where the fabric was soaked through.

"And I found our first book of nursery rhymes in one of those little boxes over there."

Dixie's eyes widened. "Did you find anything inside?" She stood and walked over to look at the book while Rock observed the teapot. She only looked at the table of contents to see which rhymes were listed in the book. She was interested to see if it contained all the ones they'd found so far.

"Let's go talk to Siobhan to see if this is supposed to be here before we get too excited about it."

Rock took the lead in interviewing Siobhan. He asked about her movements after she put Hope to bed and what she did when she found out she was missing. Siobhan was a lot like

Brenda. He could tell she was upset but it wasn't effecting her nearly as much as it should be.

Because it was a standard question and because he wasn't ready to give up on a male being their prime suspect, he asked her about Hope's father.

"He's still around. We're not together, but he's come to see her a few times and he gives me money every time he gets paid."

"We'll need his contact information. And one last question, and by far the most important. Over the past few weeks, have you had anyone pay special attention to Hope? Someone you may have just met when you were out running errands or maybe while you took her on a stroll through the park? Anyone at all that you can think of, would be really helpful to us."

Siobhan shook her head a stared at the table for a moment. "I can't think of anyone off the top of my head, but when you have a newborn, everyone is interested. It's like people are drawn to the stroller. They can't wait to see the baby's face. They want to know their name, sex, and age. They want to tell you all about their child when they were that age. If I'm going to be honest, it's pretty exhausting. I'm just trying to focus on my own baby, you know?"

"I can actually relate to that very well."

They went back to the station to file their paperwork and wait until an appropriate time to go visit Marco, Siobhan's friend.

Marco worked in a warehouse not too far from the station. Siobhan had told them he worked an early shift but they waited until after eight to go speak to him. The security guard paged him over the intercom from the front desk after asking for identification. Dixie and Rock happily obliged and stood waiting for nearly fifteen minutes. Rock was tempted to go look around back, thinking he may have run, when Marco walked through the door. He was young with light brown, mop-like hair. He wore jeans and a pair of work boots with a gray t-shirt and had a badge hanging around his neck.

"Hey. Sorry. I usually work in the far end of the warehouse. It takes a few minutes to get up here. Are you here about Hope?"

Rock motioned for him to follow him. He wanted to get out of earshot of the security guard. "I take it Siobhan called you?"

"She did. Honestly, I feel kinda bad because I didn't really know how to react."

He nodded his head. "How's your relationship with Siobhan?"

"It's good. I mean, it's different since she found out she was pregnant. We weren't ever really a couple. Just friends with benefits. But we still get along and still see each other."

"And Hope? Do you spend a lot of time with her?"

"Kind of. But that's why I said I feel kinda bad. Like, I feel like I should be torn apart by what happened. Maybe it just hasn't hit me yet but, I don't know. I guess I just don't feel as upset about it as I should."

"It may take some time for the reality to sink in. How much time do you spend with the two of them?"

"I try to spend time with both of them as often as I can. I don't really know what to do with a child, being around Hope makes me a little uncomfortable. I never wanted kids. But I also didn't want to be that asshole that walks away because of it."

Dixie curled down her lips and nodded. "That says a lot about your character."

"I'm trying to be a part of her life. I don't know how I'm doing, but I'm trying."

Rock took over again. "Can you tell us where you were last night?"

"Yeah, sure. I actually had dinner at Siobhan's. I ordered Chinese takeout on my way over. We ate and watched a movie and then I went home when she said she needed to put Hope to bed."

"What time was that?"

"Mmm. I probably left her house around seven-thirty. I get to work early so I'm usually in bed by nine."

"Marco, we thank you for your time. We'll be in touch if we need anything else."

"Great." He scrunched up his face and his cheeks turned pink. "I'm sorry, that was weird. Feel free to stop by if you think I can help."

"We will." Rock fought the smile threatening his lips.

Walking out to the parking lot, Dixie looked up at Rock. "So, what'd you think?"

Rock let out a quiet laugh. "I think he was embarrassingly honest. If he's ever so much as accidentally stolen a pen without bringing it back, I'd be surprised. There's no way he took a child."

"That's what I was thinking."

Halfway back to the station, Dixie's phone rang. Rock listened to her say "Uh huh," about thirty-five times before she said "We'll head over," and hung up.

"That was Siobhan. She said she remembers someone who gave them a lot of attention."

"A woman?"

"Yup."

Rock turned at the next light and headed toward her apartment.

"Thank you for calling." Rock sat down at the kitchen table with Dixie beside him. "I'm going to let you do most of the talking, just tell us what happened, why she sticks out in your mind, and give us as many details as you can about her."

"Okay, um. Well, like I told you, a lot of people want to talk to you when you have a baby. But I thought about it after you left and this one lady popped into my head. I was in the park, taking Hope for a walk. I sat on a bench so we could enjoy the sunshine for a while because it was nice outside."

"What day was this?"

"Um, three days ago? So, Tuesday? We were just about to leave when this lady sat down next to us. She ignored Hope at first and started talking about the weather and how nice it was. And then she reached her hand into Hope's stroller and moved her blanket so she could see her face. I think that's the main reason I remember her, because a lot of people touch the stroller but I've never had someone reach their whole hand in there before. We went through the typical questions: age, name, whatever. But then, instead of assuming I was married like most do, she actually asked me if I was a single mother. Aside from just being rude, it's really none of a stranger's business."

"What did you tell her?"

"I just told her I wasn't married but her dad was a big part of her life. I may have stretched the truth a little but I didn't really care. But then, she started asking where I lived and what I did for a living and I wasn't really comfortable answering those questions so I made up an excuse about having to put Hope down for a nap and I left."

"What happened after that?"

"Well, I came straight home and locked my door behind me. But after I walked away, I turned back to look at her once and she was gone. The park was kind of busy but it seemed like she just vanished."

"Do you remember what she looked like?"

"Kind of. She had really light brown eyes, almost more of a tan color. Her hair was brown and looked really dry. And she was all bundled up, more like she was dressed for a late fall walk than a summer one. She was wearing a jacket and big, bulky scarves. That's another reason I think I remember her. Because I questioned why she was dressed like that. For a split second, I almost thought she might be homeless but realized her scarves were actually probably a little expensive and she looked too clean. I could smell her laundry detergent when the wind blew."

"Did you tell her where you lived?"

"No. Not really. I told her I didn't live too far from the park." Her eyes began to gloss over. "You don't think she followed me home, do you?" Worry crept over her face and Dixie knew she was blaming herself for what happened to Hope.

"No, we don't think she did. Even with a lot of people in the park that day, you would have noticed her if she was following you based on how you described her clothing. Did anything else stand out to you? Tattoos, piercings, the sound of her voice? Anything that could distinguish her from others?"

"Nothing that I can remember."

"Okay. Thank you for calling and for taking the time to talk to us again. We know you're going through a lot right now and we really appreciate your cooperation. If you think of anything else, no matter how trivial it may seem, please call us."

"I will." Siobhan stood and walked them out, locking the door behind them.

Rock and Dixie set out to enjoy a late morning stroll through the park. This must have been the same type of weather Siobhan had enjoyed while she was there. The sun was warm and there was a cool breeze circling around. The sky was bright blue with light, puffy clouds floating overhead. They started at the far end and made their way through the small patch of trees, watching all the benches and keeping an eye out for any women with strollers. They wanted to keep moving forward but progress was slow as the park was busy again. Almost all the benches they passed were full. Some people were enjoying the weather, listening to music, some were scrolling idly through their cell phones. A few people were reading newspapers or magazines. People had blankets spread out over the grass and were reading books or typing on their laptops. But the majority were doing the same thing they were, just walking. It was hard to say whether they were enjoying the scenery or just passing through.

The far end of the park had a stone water fountain with an angel perched on top. It signified the beginning of a flower garden that was maintained by a local volunteer group. It covered almost three quarters of an acre and was home to over a thousand plant and flower varieties. The local group often held tours throughout the summer, asking for donations in exchange, but it was free to the public to walk around in at their will. Aside from having just a garden, the group had dedicated space to various scenes where they created elaborate landscapes to showcase a few of their favorite varieties.

At the fountain, the cement walkway veered off into four separate paths and Rock and Dixie split up so they could cover as much ground as possible. With all the stress they had been feeling and the thought that they may be running out of time, both of them wanted to slow down and enjoy the views the garden offered. Numerous times they both had to remind themselves that they needed to focus on the people. It took almost forty-five minutes to make it back to their meeting spot at the fountain. Dixie walked around the front to see Rock sitting on the edge, dipping his fingers in the water.

"You taking a little break there, Rock?" Dixie laughed and sat down beside him.

"You know, I was just thinking. I dated this girl once, well, I didn't really date her, it was more of a one night stand I think. I can't remember where I was but I know it was in a hotel so I was probably on vacation. Anyway, we were at a bar drinking, we got to talking, and one thing led to another as they tend to do. We went back to her room and did our thing and fell asleep. I remember waking up and seeing her curled up in the chair, under the wall lamp, reading a book. But it wasn't a normal book like a novel. Under the light I could see the cover shining. It was a big coffee table book... of nursery rhymes. Even in my state of half-drunkenness and being half-asleep, I remember thinking how odd it was that a grown woman was reading nursery rhymes. It made me uncomfortable."

Dixie watched him intently as he spoke. This was the first time he had really opened up to her about anything personal. "Did you ask her about it?"

"No. She heard me stir and she held up the book and said 'It's comforting, I've had the book since I was little,' I left before she got up in the morning. I had completely forgotten about it until just a little while ago, after I started walking through the garden. There was a little gnome that I walked by that reminded me of the cover of the book. I'm sure it sounds stupid but I think with the case, it made me remember. What I can't remember is her face or her name."

"That's not unusual." She giggled just a little bit. "I mean, to be fair, that's how I would describe a good half of my partners." She backtracked. "That sounds really bad. It's not actually what I meant but I think you get the point."

"I do. I just think it's weird that I've had that experience and I'm working a case with nursery rhyme clues. How many people would be able to claim either of those situations, let alone both?"

"Probably no one else on the planet. I understand why you would be a little put off by it but I think it really is just an odd coincidence. I mean, how long ago was this? It has to be at least a couple of years, right?"

"You're probably right. I've been with Jill for almost six years now so it had to have been at least that long ago."

They enjoyed the fountain for a few more minutes in silence before Rock stood up. "It's starting to get a little late. We should make our way back to the station."

Dixie joined him and they continued in their fruitless effort to find a homely woman reaching into strangers' strollers on their way back to the car.

Dixie went home that evening and showered and made dinner. Her cat, Pinecone, curled up next to her on the couch. Dixie scratched her behind her ears and relaxed at the innocent sound of the mellow purr coming from her throat. If only life was as simple for her as it was for her cat. The ability to appreciate the small things had become harder over the years and she was finding it more and more difficult to let things happen without her being in control. Starting at around eight years old, her mother had come to depend on her to take care of herself and her brother. Being raised in a single parent household, her mom was good to them when they were young, but as soon as they were old enough to fend for themselves, all the kindness and care stopped. The lived on cereal and sandwiches for most of their meals and their mother, when she came home from work, usually changed and left again for the evening, leaving them to complete their homework, bathe, and get ready for bed. When Dixie turned sixteen, she got her first job so she could save money for a car and she purchased food that actually had to be cooked. She saved money so Branden could go on school field trips that they'd never been able to take part in before. She wanted to give him a chance to experience things that she had never, herself, been able to.

Branden became dependent on her at a young age and struggled with her leaving him to work her part time job. He was lacking the necessary social skills to find friends of his own and was becoming disruptive at school. Twice within a year's time, an agent from the department of Children and Families visited their home because of his behavior. It was Dixie who had to convince them they were okay. Because of her work and the dedication she put into keeping them a family, the agents found a clean house, clean, clothed children, and cabinets full of food. Her mother never thanked her or showed any appreciation for what she did.

Dixie wanted to leave as soon as she turned eighteen but couldn't bring herself to leave Branden alone in the house. It wasn't until he got arrested for petty larceny shortly after he turned sixteen that Dixie decided she needed to leave for good. Their mother had all but moved out of the house, stopping by only briefly to change her clothes or eat some food. She acted more like an estranged child than a parent, but the bills were paid and Dixie knew she could leave Branden in the house safely without having to worry about the basic things. For the next six months, she stopped by the house once a week to bring him food and leave him some money in case he needed anything extra. On her last visit to the house, she found her mother curled up on the sofa wearing a bathrobe and struggling to stay awake. She learned that Branden had left hours after she saw him last and hadn't been home since. Dixie was just shy of being twenty-one years old and she hadn't spoken to her mother since that day. She blamed her for Branden leaving and her mother never denied it. Neither of them ever tried to reconcile the relationship with their mother.

Having been in control of most aspects of her life for as long as she could remember, Dixie found it necessary to hand over the reins and relinquish power every once in a while. The friends she called up every few weeks were the ones she chose to hand the reigns to. She was familiar with the men she called and she chose them because she trusted them. While their visits did satisfy her sexual needs, it was less about the sex and more about the physical closeness and lack of power. It was an intimacy on a different level. Dixie had only had one serious relationship about ten years ago and after seven months she felt like she was losing control. They tried to talk about it and tried to work through it but she couldn't do it. She didn't like having someone constantly around her, touching her things, interfering with her schedule. She preferred being able to call up a friend when she was feeling lonely or overworked and letting them take care of her, knowing they would go home afterwards.

She called her friend Steve and asked him to come visit. She had been trying to relax but she was restless. She also wanted something to take her mind off the possibility that she was pregnant. Steve told her he would be over within the hour but he wanted her to wait to get changed. That was the last thing Dixie expected and she was worried about what he would say to her.

When he got to her house, she let him in and struggled to keep her hands to herself as he led her over to the couch. Dixie drank in his chocolate eyes and dark brown hair. Not a single strand of gray showed though and she wished she was that lucky. His frame was much larger than hers, he stood at nearly six feet, two inches and his muscles were taut. He had tossed her around the bed like a ragdoll on numerous occasions. "I promise I won't keep you waiting too long. But I wanted to talk to you for a minute to see how you were feeling. You've called me an awful lot over the last few weeks since you've been here and I thought you might want to talk about it."

This wasn't what Dixie was expecting. When he said he wanted to talk beforehand, she thought for sure he was going to call their relationship off or tell her he was moving back to Georgia. Steve was a private investigator and he and Dixie had been friends for years. He was also looking for something new in his life so when Dixie told him she was moving, he asked if it was okay for him to follow her. She obliged willingly and couldn't be happier that he wanted to move with her. He wasted no time getting his license to practice in other states and was in town less than a week after Dixie had arrived. "I guess the case might be getting to me a little bit. The ones involving a mother and child always affect me a little more than others. But it's also weird to not be home. Not that I ever felt like I was home anywhere but at least in Georgia I knew people."

"What else is bothering you?" He saw her shake her head but he wasn't going to let it go that easily. "Dixie, look at me." He cupped her chin in his hand gently drew her head up. "I can see it in your eyes. You can't hide from me."

Her eyes stung with tears. "My brother. As always."

"Is he okay?"

"I'm not sure. I saw him early last week but I haven't heard from him since he left. And, of course, he did not leave of his own free will."

Steve nodded his head "Typical. Do you want my help finding him? Just so you know he's okay?"

Dixie shook her head. "No. The last thing I want is for more people watching him. I think he has enough already. And, there's something else. Someone is watching me, us, my partner. I can't really go into detail but the last time you were here, they took pictures of us through the window and delivered them to my partner. You couldn't see our faces. But, the pictures showed... things. And..." She took a few breaths and blew them out slowly before gathering up the courage to tell him. "I think I might be pregnant." She closed her eyes not wanting to see the look on his face.

"Ah. Whose is it?"

Dixie shrugged her shoulders, not having the courage to speak.

Steve stood and grabbed her hand, leading her to the bedroom where he picked her up and tossed her onto the bed.

She looked at him with desire burning in her eyes.

He held her gaze, looking deep into her eyes. He wanted so desperately to tell her how in love with her he was, but couldn't bring himself to risk what they had.

Chapter VII

This may be the easiest one yet. She runs her house like clockwork. Every day it's the same routine, the same time. Her door is never locked. They could see it, wide open, through the ground floor window, inviting them in.

Dixie's phone rang and she stirred. An unfamiliar weight was drawing her back. She turned her head to the side and realized it was Steve's arm wrapped around her waist, pulling her close. She groaned and reached for her phone. "I'll be there as soon as I can." She hung up and peeled his arm off her bare skin. She sat up and rubber her eyes, wondering how they had both managed to fall asleep. Steve often stayed until she fell asleep from pure, physical exhaustion but he had never stayed long enough to sleep himself.

She nudged his shoulder with the palm of her hand and he gathered her in his arms again. She slapped his shoulder this time to get his attention. He slowly opened his eyes and looked at her. "I have to go. New kidnapping. You can stay the night. Just lock up when you leave okay?" She kissed him on the cheek as she did often and scrambled out from underneath the covers to get dressed.

She greeted Rock within fifteen minutes but barely had the energy to speak. "I'm too tired for this shit," she stated matter of factly.

"Tell me about it. For once, I was sleeping well. My wife actually had to wake me up to tell me my phone was ringing. I wake up when the wind blows."

"Right? I don't think I've had a good night's sleep in years. I wake up constantly all night long."

"So, what do you think we're walking into tonight? Hysterical woman who claims she was holding the baby when it was taken?" To outsiders, his statement would seem cold and uncaring but it was the little jokes like this that allowed detectives to keep their sanity. No matter how hard they tried, they always became emotionally invested in every case, good or bad.

"Hmm." Dixie tapped her chin dramatically like she was thinking hard about it. "No. I'm thinking immaculate conception. Thirty year old claiming to still be a virgin. A miracle birth and a savior that came to show the child the right path."

Rock laughed out loud and it echoed around the full, still parking lot. "I didn't expect you to take it quite that far. Let's see what we drew out of the hat tonight."

"I hope it's a bunny. I could use a cuddly, furry friend right about now."

When they walked in, they were pleasantly surprised to find Gemini's team already there. They had waited for Rock and Dixie before entering the nursery as a professional courtesy. The detectives always wanted to see the scene first to be able to compare it to the others. Gemini gave them both a look of warning and they followed her eyes over to Jessica. She was wearing a pair of dress slacks and a blouse. She was much older than they expected her to be and the look on her face told them exactly what Gemini was warning them about. She didn't seem to be upset at all about the kidnapping itself but she was clearly livid about having so many people in her apartment. Not willing to deal with her quite yet, Rock led the way into the nursery.

Dixie was immediately taken in with the decor consisting of stars covering the walls and bed linens. There were two stuffed star pillows on the rocking chair and the room was covered in deep blues and silvers. It immediately calmed her.

The dresser and crib were painted a lighter blue and had decal stars placed along the drawers, legs, and bars. It was a good thing the kidnapper chose a different person to use the Twinkle, Twinkle Little Star rhyme with because no one would have noticed any extra stars in this room. They were everywhere, big, small, everything was covered with them. The nursery was like its own magical universe. On the corner of the crib, a garden hose nozzle was tied in place to the post and a stuffed spider dangled just below. On the wall closest to Dixie, a silver, wooden star was fastened to the wall and the bingo ball sat in one of the inside points, sorely out of place with the rest of the room. Dixie leaned down to look under the dresser and noticed the other thing out of place was the carpet, no doubt much too expensive to replace. It was a dull brown and scratchy material that looked as though it had been there as long as the building had been standing.

The window on the side wall, like the rest, was locked from the inside and the valance was made of a clear, shimmery material with dangling stars of various sizes hanging from it. "I need a room in my house like this. It's soothing."

Rock gave her a sideways glance, thinking she might be a bit insane.

"Well, minus the crib and stuff. But look at how pretty it is. I bet the entire room lights up when they lights are off."

Rock shrugged and walked to the light switch to turn them off. Just as Dixie predicted, the room was almost as bright as when the lights were on. The ceiling had a glowing solar system and shooting stars covered every corner of the room. Even Rock was awed by the aesthetic.

They went out to interview Jessica and she was exactly as they had suspected when they walked in. They took turns asking questions and went through all the basics. When Dixie asked for a walk through of her evening, Jessica responded curtly.

"I put Madeline to bed. I went to bed. I don't see how this is relevant."

They asked about Madeline's father and were faced with the same type of response.

"I have no idea. I told him I was pregnant and he disappeared. Changed his phone number and everything."

"Can we have his name?"

"Ryan Curtis."

"Do you know where he works?"

"City Edge Motel. He does maintenance." She rolled her eyes and shifted in her chair, letting them know she was ready for the conversation to be over.

"Have you tried to go see him there since he changed his number?"

"Now, why would I do that? If he doesn't want to be a part of our lives, I'm certainly not going to waste my time trying to force him to be."

"That's fair. One last question and then we'll leave you alone."

Jessica huffed and rolled her eyes again.

"Did you notice anyone in the past couple of days that was paying extra attention to Madeline maybe when you took her out to a park or to run some errands?"

"Detective, I'm not sure if you've noticed or not, but I'm not really one for small talk. And people have to go through me to get to my daughter. So, no, no one gave her too much attention."

"Okay. We'll be in touch."

They walked out to the parking lot both shaking their heads and wondering how they keep finding these women. Rock was feeling a bit punchy and walked his fingers up the back of Dixie's neck and it made her shiver. "Itsy, Bitsy Spider." He laughed.

Dixie stopped walking and turned around and punched him in the arm.

"Ouch. Damn, you know how to hit."

"Lucky for me I don't have to stay professional when it's dark outside and no one can see me. That gave me goosebumps."

"I might have a new theory."

"Oh, yeah? What's your theory?"

"I wonder if maybe it's not the babies that we should be looking for a connection with, but the women."

Dixie looked at him with her eyes squinted. "What makes you say that?"

"Well, think about it. Think about all the women we've met so far and think about their personalities. We've met, what, two so far that have been relatively nice? And not only that but most of them barely even seem to care that their child is missing. I feel like the only reason some of them even called is because they knew they had to."

Dixie nodded her head and got into her car. He might not be wrong but she needed a few minutes to think about it. When she got to the station she walked in and flopped into her chair. "I am so tired. But, I think you might be on to something. I'm just not quite sure what it is. It could go back to the kidnapper not thinking the women deserve the children. Maybe it is that carefree attitude they all have that's the problem. On an individual basis, we could look at almost any one of them and question whether they had something to do with their daughter's disappearance. I mean, it doesn't make much sense since there are a number of them now but if it was only one."

"You're babbling. But I understand what you're saying. Maybe we try that angle for a while and see what we get from it?"

"No. I mean, part of it could be that but I don't think it's all there is. Are you convinced yet that we're looking for a woman?"

"Not even a little bit. What Henry said makes sense. I get what he's saying. But I'm just struggling to believe that a woman is capable of this. It doesn't make any sense that, as a woman, she would deny the right of motherhood to any woman, regardless of how she may feel about them personally. If she even knows them personally." He fidgeted with a stack of paperwork on his desk. "You're like a woman.

Would you ever be able to take someone's child away from them?"

Dixie laughed at his absurd comment. "Yeah. Last I checked I actually *am* a woman. Hard to believe, I know." She grinned at him. "But, no. I would never be able to take a woman's baby away from her. Then again, I'm also not a psychopath."

Rock scrunched up his face. "Yeah, I guess I should take that part into consideration. I'm not saying I'm not going to look at women as potential suspects but I'm not going to stop looking at men either. I don't think we have enough proof either way to justify a definitive gender. Shit, we don't have any proof of anything at this point."

Dixie didn't hear a word he said. As soon as she made the comment about not being able to take a woman's child away from them, her mind immediately went back to her potential situation. The one good thing about getting another call was that it took her mind off her own problems for a while. She had never wanted children. She spent too much time taking care of her brother. She did it because she loved him but also because she had to. Someone had to. The truth was, like her own mother, Dixie didn't have that motherly instinct. She didn't get all gushy when she saw a baby or a pregnant woman. She didn't care to see pictures of people's kids. It just wasn't a part of who she was. Now that she was facing the possibility of having a child, she was terrified. She had no idea what she was going to do.

Rock's phone buzzed and he looked at the screen. His eyes narrowed and he picked it up from his desk. "It's my wife."

Dixie saw his face change from confusion to concern as he listened intently to what she was saying.

"Okay. Slow down. Can you see what's in it? Don't touch it. Just see if you can see anything from the window." He waited for her to look at something and respond back. "Okay. Stay in the house. We'll be there soon." He hung up the phone and stood up. "Let's go."

With no hesitation, Dixie jumped up and followed him out the door. Rock was practically sprinting through the parking lot talking to someone on his phone. He was in the car with it started and in drive before Dixie even reached for the door handle. She hopped in and he sped away before she could fasten her seatbelt. "Stone has the bomb squad going out to my place."

Dixie's eyes widened and she slowly turned her head to look at him. "What?"

"My wife called to tell me there is a basket of stuff sitting on our front step. It wasn't there when I left. Stone said he's unwilling to take any chances and he's sending the bomb squad out as a precaution. I'm trying to get there before they do so my wife doesn't completely lose her mind."

"Oh no. Did she say what was in the basket? Did she get a good look at it?"

"No. She went back inside as soon as she saw it and couldn't see anything through the window."

"How does she know it isn't a legitimate gift? Like a belated baby gift or something?"

Rock took a deep breath. "Because her eye only caught one thing. It was a picture of Ella."

"Oh." Dixie remained silent for the rest of the ride. As they pulled up to the house, the bomb squad was just making their way up the street. Rock slammed on his brakes in the middle of the road and threw open his door. "Stop." He put his hand up and ran across the street. "Detective Rockefeller. This is my house. Please. Let me go around back and get my wife. She's probably terrified seeing your van over there. I have an infant inside as well."

The bomb tech paused for a moment and then nodded his head. "I'll go first. Is the door unlocked?"

"Uh, no. It shouldn't be."

The technician put out his hand for the key.

Dixie stood in the middle of the driveway. She didn't want to interfere. Her heart was pounding from the anxiety of there possibly being a bomb close by. She was fine with guns and knives because she knew it was always possible, albeit slim, to survive an interaction with one. But a bomb was a bomb. Everything around it would be gone if it blew. It seemed like a lifetime before she saw Rock come around the side of the house with his arm wrapped around his wife, holding the baby.

"Dixie, take my wife down to the end of the road that way. I'll call you when it's safe to come back."

Dixie nodded and put her arm around his wife and guided her to the car. She opened the passenger door until she was settled and ran around to the driver's side. "They're professionals. It'll be okay. It's just a precaution because of that person that's been leaving Rock notes." She patted her on the knee and pulled the car ahead.

Forty-five minutes went by, the seconds gruelingly ticking away. They couldn't see the house from where they were parked and there had been no communication from Rock or Stone. Dixie's phone rang out and both of them jumped. Ella started crying, probably more from the physical jolt than the noise.

"All clear. You can come back now. How's my wife?"

"A little on edge. That felt like a lifetime." She ended the call and put the car in drive before turning to his wife. "It's all clear. We can go back to the house." She watched as her eyes filled with tears of relief and she saw her arms wrap a little tighter around her daughter. She stared for a few seconds wondering if she would feel that same love toward a child. Shaking her head to refocus, she drove back to the house. Rock met them at the car and opened the passenger door. He reached in and took his daughter from his wife's arms. Dixie met him around that side of the car and without hesitating he handed Ella to Dixie so he could hug his wife. Dixie's jaw dropped and she reluctantly put her arms out to take the child. Ella looked up at her and then rested her head in the crook of her shoulder. Dixie just stood there, nearly paralyzed from the idea of holding a child. Her throat tightened and her mouth watered. She could feel the bile rising and she closed her eyes and took a few deep breaths to calm herself.

"Dixie!"

The power in Rock's voice startled her and she opened her eyes.

"Jesus, I thought you were sleeping standing up. I'll take Ella back now." He reached out his arms and claimed his baby.

"I'm sorry. I may have been a little bit. I didn't really get any sleep last night, you know?"

"I'm right there with you. I feel like I could sleep for a week."

Dixie nodded. "So, I'm glad to hear the basket was a false alarm. Can I ask what was in it?"

Before Rock could answer, Stone approached the trio. "Mrs. Rockefeller, we'd like to ask you a few questions about this morning."

"Oh, I already told Larry everything I know." She sounded so innocent and still so scared.

"That's okay. He's a little too close to the situation and we'd like to talk to you ourselves." He gestured for her to lead the way into the house and he nodded at Dixie and Rock.

When he walked away Rock finally answered Dixie's question. "The weirdest thing. Everything in the basket was exactly what the person has already left on my car. Almost like they didn't think I had told her and they wanted to do it themselves. The only thing missing was the note about you. Uh," he cleared his throat, "your pictures were there but the note wasn't."

Dixie pursed her lips. "Maybe they wanted her to think there was more to it than showing you pictures of your partner's dirty little secrets."

He dug his phone out of his pocket and slammed his fingers onto the touchscreen. "I almost forgot."

"What's the matter?"

"Hold on." He swiped and stopped, swiped and stopped. "I almost forgot I put a camera on the window sill in the living room. If they came right up to the front door, there's no way I didn't get them on camera." His face scrunched up and Dixie could see his muscles tightening. "There's no way. It's not possible. How?"

Dixie reached out and took the phone from his hand. She pulled the time back on the video and watched as just a shoulder appeared briefly on the screen and then disappeared. That was it. She scrolled further along in the video and there was nothing else. "They must know there's a camera there. It's the only way they could miss it." She ran up to the house and looked behind the bushes that lined the front of it. She crouched and leaned forward, looking for any sign of footprints in the bedding around the shrubs. Seeing nothing, she stood up and shook her head. "I don't see anything but they must have come over with their back to the front of the house."

Rock was pacing across the driveway chewing on the side of his finger.

Dixie went over and put her hand on his shoulder to stop him from moving. "I'm guessing Stone doesn't know about that camera?"

He shook his head. "No. I wanted some part of my life to remain private. Now, he's inside my house, talking to my wife, probably holding my daughter. And now I have to tell him I put a camera up that he didn't know about. I can almost guarantee he's going to be camped outside my house for the next week watching through a pair of binoculars."

Dixie curled her lips. "I really want to argue with you but you're probably right. I will tell you I'd have the same reaction if he was going to do it to me. But since I'm on the other end of it, you know if he does it, it's for your own good. I don't think he cares enough about what you do in your personal time but he does care about your well-being and that of your family. You can't hold that against him."

"I know."

The front door flew open and the lead bomb technician followed Stone out. "Your wife wants to see you."

Dixie gave Rock a half-hearted smile. "I'll catch a ride back to the station with Stone."

Rock took the rest of the day off. Dixie spend the majority of the day switching back and forth between filling out paperwork and staring at the white board hoping for a miracle to appear before her that connected everything. She added the new residence to the map along with the bingo ball number. She tried running the string between the locations to see if the central location had changed but they still crossed at the same block. Rock had sent her a message a few hours ago to tell her that he called Stone about the camera. She had tried to avoid him since then so she didn't get sucked into the middle. Now, she tapped on his door before stepping inside his office. "I'm going to take off for the night. I'll stop at the lab on my way home to pick up the scene pictures and see if Gemini has anything to tell us from this morning."

Stone nodded his head without looking up. "Ask her to stop by Rock's on her way home to check up on him and his wife."

"You got it." Dixie left before he could start any other conversation with her.

Stopping at the lab didn't require much of her time, Gemini didn't have any information to give her so Dixie picked up the photos, relayed Stone's request, and left. She was exhausted and wasn't really up for any conversation other than work. When she got home, she didn't bother to make dinner. She curled up in bed with the television on and promptly fell asleep.

It was nearly seven when Gemini pulled into Rock's driveway. She had been there a few times over the years for various occasions. She was friendly with his wife once she assured her that their relationship was strictly professional. She liked Jill but found she could be a bit untrusting at times. Gemini understood where Rock came from on that front. She knocked on the door quietly, hoping Ella was still awake but trying not to wake her if she wasn't. Rock answered the door and opened it wide for her to step in.

He smiled. "I'm guessing you're not here of your own will?"

"Good guess. Your boss sent me. Better me than him though, right?"

"Always. Can I get you a drink?"

"No. I won't stay long. I actually did want to check in on you anyway but I probably would have called. Stone asked me to stop by so I'm here. How are you?"

"More pissed off than anything else. My wife is pretty upset. I don't suppose..."

Gemini smiled at him. "I'll talk to her."

"I owe you. We were just going to have a quick dessert. There's coffee and a homemade lemon Bundt cake in the kitchen. I'll send her in and I'll put Ella to bed. Thank you for coming over."

Rock disappeared down the hallway and Gemini made her way to the kitchen where she filled up two coffee cups and was just setting them on the table when Jill walked in. She looked visibly worn. Her shoulders were slumped and her face was void of any makeup. She had dark shadows under her eyes and her movements were slow.

"Hi", she greeted Gemini while she grabbed the cake from the counter.

"Hi. I'll get that. You sit down." She placed her hand under the plate and eased it from Jill's grip. "How are you feeling?"

She pulled out a chair and sat down, rubbing her forehead. "I've been better. It's very unnerving to know that someone is watching everything you do. Even worse with an infant to worry about."

"Mhm. Rock has been keeping you informed whenever he's gotten any communication from this person, right?" With two plates and forks in hand, she joined her at the table.

"He has. At least, I think he's told me about every time." She placed a piece of cake on one of the plates and slid it across to Gemini.

"Thank you. I know this morning was tough for you because you probably didn't expect to see the bomb squad pull up in front of your house. To be honest, even when I know they're coming to a scene it still makes me uneasy. Aside from that part of it, what is it about what happened today that made it so hard for you?"

She looked at her with the fork half way to her mouth and her mouth hanging open. "I'm not sure what you mean."

Gemini took a sip of her coffee and cringed at how hot it was. "I mean, you already knew about the messages that Rock was getting. So why did it hit you so hard today? It is because it may have been directed more towards you or maybe because you saw it firsthand rather than just hearing about it?"

She stared at the table unsure of how to respond. "I guess, maybe both of those things. I was a little nervous, usually on the days that he got a message, but that was it. I just took extra precautions, you know, locking all the doors while I was home, making sure no one was following us while we were out. Stuff I probably should do anyway. But now, it feels real. It feels personal. I don't even want to walk in front of the windows because I feel like someone is out there watching every step I take." She laid her fork on her plate and rested her arms on the table. "I feel helpless, like I wouldn't be able to protect Ella if someone actually showed their face."

Gemini nodded her head in confirmation as she listened to her talk. "Your feelings are perfectly reasonable. But I will tell you, the chances of anyone coming to you would be slim. Based on what I can tell, they want Rock to hear what they're saying. It could be an old girlfriend of his or just an admirer. It's possible it's an old boyfriend of yours that wants Rock out of the way. Either way, I don't believe they are looking to hurt you or Ella. At least not physically."

"That doesn't make me feel better knowing they're after him."

"Well, no. The initial thought doesn't sound very comforting but you have to remember, he carries a gun. He's around police officers all day long and his partner is always with him. He has protection around him all the time." She put her hand out and laid it on top of his wife's. "I also don't believe anyone is intending to harm him. It's his attention they want. I've looked at every photo and every note they've left. Not one of them shows any intention of harm."

"So what am I supposed to do? Sit in the house all day and hope I don't get a phone call telling me something terrible has happened to him?"

"No, not at all. You keep doing what you've always done. You get up in the morning and run errands and take Ella to the park. You act like nothing is any different than it was, because it isn't. I know this morning was hard for you but the same thing has been happening for the last four months since Ella was born. You can't let it stop you from living your life."

His wife just stared at her not knowing if she should believe her or not.

"Trust me. You'll be safe. Stone has a crew set up to watch your house. I saw the plain clothes officer keeping watch when I pulled up your street earlier."

"Really?"

"Really. Rock's pretending to not be happy about it but I know him pretty well and I know he feels much better knowing someone is looking out for you."

Rock walked into the kitchen and poured himself a cup of coffee. "Ella's sleeping."

Gemini stood up and placed her plate and mug in the sink. "I think I'm going to head out. Rock, I'll talk to you tomorrow. Jill, thank you for your hospitality. The cake was wonderful. Please, don't hesitate to call me if you need to chat. Rock will give you my number."

"Thank you," she replied with tears stinging her eyes. She was always thankful for Gemini. She had such a calming effect on everyone whenever she was around.

Rock's phone woke him at four thirty the next morning. He wasn't expecting to be woken up so early two days in a row. He prayed the kidnapper wasn't upping their game and going back to back nights. His voice sounded gruff when he answered the phone. "Rockefeller."

"Which one of you do I owe thanks to for leaking this to the press?"

He sat up and cleared his throat. "You'll have to forgive me, Captain, it's barely after four in the morning. What are we talking about?"

"Your friend, Leila, over at the newspaper. She wrote up a neat little story about you and your stalker."

"Ha. And you think I told her to do it? I don't even want you to know about it."

"I'm going to ignore that last statement. And yes, either you or your partner. No one else knows."

"Gemini knows." His retort was louder than he intended and Jill stirred in bed. "And she's just as likely to leak the information as Dixie and I are."

"Gemini knows better."

"So do we."

"Fine. Just, go talk to Leila and find out where she got her information from."

"I'll call Dixie and have her meet me over there." He hung up before Stone had a chance to reply. He got dressed and left the bedroom so he didn't wake his wife. He pulled up the article and mumbled under his breath as he read. "I'm going to kill her. I'm a detective and I'm going to end up in prison for murder." Before giving in to the urge to throw his phone across the room, he closed out of the article and called Dixie.

"Hey. What are you doing up so early?" Her voice was chipper and Rock had to look at his phone to make sure he called the right person.

"Were you... already awake?"

"Yeah. I've been up for about an hour now. I crashed as soon as I got home yesterday."

"How nice for you. Can you meet me at the news station in about twenty minutes? Seems our friend Leila has been busy."

"Oh, shit. Not again."

"Again. This time Stone thinks you told her about my stalker." He pulled the phone away from his head waiting for her to scream into the mouthpiece.

"Why me? That mother..." She growled into the phone. "Give me twenty-five."

They stood at the front desk of the news station. Rock was impatiently tapping his foot, knowing Leila was purposely taking her time to come talk to them.

"What do you want detectives? Isn't it a little early for you two to be whining about how well I do my job?"

They both turned to see her walking down the hallway. She had a smug look on her face and rock wanted to reach out and slap it off. He had never considered hitting a woman before but she made his blood boil.

"Who told you about what happened yesterday?" His voice bellowed down the hall.

"I'm so glad you've taken an interest in reading my articles. It's always nice to meet my fans." Her cherry lipstick glistened in the overhead lights and made her smile look vicious.

"I will never be your fan. Now can you answer my question?"

She raised one eyebrow at him. "I'm afraid I can't. Anonymous source."

"Do you happen to know this source that you claim is anonymous?"

"As fun as that would be for me, no. This time I actually don't. I got a message from a courier with the information."

"How did you know the information was true?"

""Well, let's see," she put her finger up to her lips like she had to think about her response. "Oh, that's right. I did my job, Detective. I drove over to your house and saw the bomb squad there. It kind of told me everything I needed to know."

"And the courier? Did you see him?"

"Nope. I don't come out to personally greet everyone. He left the message at the desk. I came out and got it when I was free."

Rock turned to the guard at the front desk. "Did you see the courier?"

"Probably. I mean, yeah, but we get people in and out of here all day. I couldn't tell you which one it was."

"Do you think maybe you could try?"

"I really don't know. I see about eight or nine of them a day. Some I see a lot. Others I see once and then never see them again."

Leila cleared her throat. "If we're done, I have real work to do. Rockefeller, I'm sure we'll talk soon. Doggie, err Dixie, is it? Have a good day."

The station was still nearly empty when they arrived. Rock couldn't stop pacing and Dixie was afraid to say anything about it. He stopped briefly and pointed at her. "Maybe we can find a judge that's willing to sign a search warrant for the message the courier delivered." He picked up his pacing again.

Dixie squinted her eyes at him. "For what, exactly?"

"If we can get the message, we could have Gemini test it for fingerprints. If she finds one, the courier might be in the system somewhere and if we can find them, we might be able to find out who sent the message."

Dixie almost laughed out loud but managed to contain her amusement. "Rock. I know this is personal to you but you know that won't ever work. There's not a judge alive that would risk his career over that far-fetched idea. I mean, the thought process is a good one but let's see if we can come up with a legal way to use that train of thought."

He sat down and vigorously tapped his pen on the desk.

Dixie could tell his mind was going one hundred miles an hour. "We'll figure something out. How many courier services are there in this area?"

"I don't know. Fifty? One hundred, maybe?"

"Please tell me you're joking." She pulled up a website on her computer and typed in "courier service near me". Seventy-eight listings showed up. "I guess you weren't." After twenty minutes of refining the search by neighborhood, she still had over twenty possible companies. "Does no one do anything themselves anymore?" She leaned back in her chair and closed her eyes. "Hey, Rock. Pull up that video from the night before last. I know it only showed what I'm guessing is a shoulder but maybe they'll be a patch or something on the shirt that we can see. Something we didn't notice the first time."

He pulled his phone out of his pocket and stared at it. "Nothing. It looks like maybe the shoulder of a sweatshirt."

"Damn. I just thought that maybe if the person hired someone to deliver the message, maybe they hired them to deliver them all, you know?"

"It makes perfect sense. I feel kind of stupid for not thinking of it myself."

They were so caught up in what they had been doing, neither of them had noticed the station filling with people. Dixie's phone rang and she looked at the screen. The number came up as blocked but she answered it anyway. "Lane." She stood and walked away from her desk. "Whoa. Slow down. Where are you? I'm at work, I can't just leave. Okay. I'll figure something out just... stay there, okay?" She ended the call and walked back to her desk. "I have an emergency. I have to go. Are you okay if I...?"

"Everything okay?"

"My brother, he's... I have to go." She grabbed her keys off the top of her desk and left without telling Stone or waiting for more questions. One of these days, Branden was going to get her fired. If not for leaving work without permission, it would be for helping a criminal with three warrants out for his arrest.

Dixie pulled up to the park and got out of her car. The sun was shining bright and she had to shield her eyes to see. The park was huge. She had no idea how she was going to find him. She pulled out her cell phone to call him before remembering he had called her from a blocked number. Most likely, he had traded in his phone and got a burner phone again so people couldn't find him. For being such a beautiful day, the park was nearly vacant. It sat on the outskirts of the city and was lined on the outside with trees. There were two sidewalks that were visible from the parking lot. One that was shaded with the trees and followed the perimeter and one that went straight through the middle. Dixie opted for the latter and started walking forward, certain there couldn't be more than one bridge in the park.

She stopped the first person she saw. "Excuse me. Could you tell me where the bridge is?"

"Which one?"

Dixie closed her eyes and sighed. "Um. How many are there?"

"Three." The woman was still jogging in place but turned and pointed. "The north bridge is that way. South is just about there and the floral bridge is about a half mile straight ahead."

"Floral?"

"Yup. I don't know if that's the official name but it's what most of us refer to it as." She nodded and took off running again.

Dixie spun around and looked in all directions. As far as she could see none of the bridges were in sight. Taking a chance and knowing her brother, she continued straight. He was probably hiding out under the floral bridge thinking it's the last place someone would look for him.

She was beginning to sweat and wished she had taken off her jacket before leaving her car. The bridge had finally come into view and she realized right away why people called it the floral bridge. It looked like it had popped out of a fantasy movie. Someone had spray painted the most colorful, beautiful flowers all along the side of it, covering all of the bricks that it was made of.

Ivy was dripping down the entire length of it so the flowers were almost hiding behind it. She made a mental note to come back when she had some time to explore because outside of the current situation, it was almost magical to see. She slowed her pace and continued her journey toward the bridge. When she got near the entrance, Branden poked his face out into the sliver of sunlight that was hitting the opening.

His hair, as usual, stuck out in impossible ways. One of his eyes had blackened and was swollen almost shut. His cheek on the other side was purple and twice the size it should be. His white t-shirt was torn and stained with dirt and blood.

"Jesus. I see you ran into a few of your friends."

"A whole group of 'em. They were very happy to see me."

"What are you doing back here so soon?"

Branden looked at the ground and then sat down with his legs crossed like a child.

Dixie couldn't decide whether she wanted to hug him or slap him from getting into so much trouble. She had no idea how one of them ended up as a detective and the other managed to find trouble everywhere he went.

"I never left, Dixie. I mean, I did leave. But then I came back. I was going to go and see you but I wanted to give it a few days to make sure no one followed me. It's a good thing I took the time because last night they found me."

"What happened?"

"They jumped me. Took every penny I had. Stole my cell phone. They probably would have killed me if two people hadn't walked around the corner when they did."

"If they took your money and your phone, how did you call me?"

"Oh." He stuck one foot in the air and wiggled his toes. "I traded with a hobo. He had a phone sitting on top of his cart and I asked him if I could have it. He traded me the phone for my shoes. Of course, he didn't tell me until after the trade that he didn't even know how to use the phone."

"Branden." She barked his name at him. "First of all, don't call them that. You probably don't even know what the word actually means. Second, you can't walk around the city with no shoes on your feet. Do you know how dangerous that is? Shit. You've had criminals chasing after you for years and you've managed to escape every time. You're going to end up dying from some fungus you picked up on the streets."

"That's not true. I'll probably die from something I picked up from this phone. You should have seen his hands. I'm pretty sure he had mushrooms growing out of the hair on his fingers."

Dixie squatted down and looked him in the eyes. "You're not sober, are you?"

He leaned forward and whispered while tapping at his hip. "They forgot to check the little pocket."

"That explains why you have so much anxious energy." She sat down beside him and wrapped her arm around his shoulders. "Little brother, what am I going to do with you?"

Branden rested his head on her shoulder and she knew he fell asleep when his breathing began to slow.

Dixie changed into a more comfortable position and leaned back against the curved inner wall of the bridge.

The sun shone bright across her face when she opened her eyes to the sound of a group of kids running past the opening. She woke Branden to tell him she would be back soon. She spent the afternoon and early evening buying him a new shirt and pair of pants. She purchased a new pair of sneakers and a first aid kit to clean up the scrape on his chin and cut on his eye. She picked up a phone card and took a few hundred dollars out of the bank. She bought dinner for both of them and joined Branden under the bridge to talk while they ate. He had come back down since falling asleep earlier in the day and she had a good hour long conversation with him about what was really happening. She hated to leave him there but knew it would be safer for her to leave before it got dark. She hugged him and kissed him on the forehead. "Take care of yourself and call me when you can, okay?"

She pulled into her driveway just after dark and rubbed her eyes. She was just about to slide her key into the lock on her front door when it swung open. She immediately stepped back and drew her gun. Sweat started to bead on her forehead and she could feel the blood rushing through every part of her body. Inching her way through the house, she paused when she heard a drawer slam shut in her bedroom. Not hearing anything else, she continued down the hallway and saw a man's silhouette in front of her nightstand.

"Police. Put your hands where I can see them."

Chapter VIII

They would have to keep an eye on this one. She was too honest for her own good and she was smart. If anyone could lead the detectives to them, it would be her.

He put his head down and raised his hands in the air. "Dixie, it's me." He turned around to face her.

Dixie lowered her gun and put her hand over her chest. "Oh, Rock. You just about scared me to death. You're lucky I didn't shoot you." Her heart was pounding, now more from relief than anxiety.

"I didn't mean to scare you. Are you okay?" He lowered his hands to his side.

"Why did you break into my house?"

"I didn't break in, the door was unlocked. But I was worried about you. You left in a hurry this morning and I tried calling you all day. Your phone went straight to voice mail again."

Dixie hung her head and stared at the floor. "I turned it off because I didn't want anyone tracing my phone. My brother is in a lot of trouble." She sat down on her bed with her body slumped.

Rock sat down next to her before realizing he had a flogger in his hand that he had dug out of her nightstand. He squinted and showed it to her. "I guess the photos really were accurate, huh?" He let out a small laugh and tried to make light of the fact that he had been rummaging around in her stuff. "I know this probably looks bad considering everything we've been dealing with the last few weeks but when I couldn't get a hold of you, I thought something might be seriously wrong."

She laughed and put one hand on his knee while gently coaxing the flogger out of his hand with the other. "You should stop playing with this." Her cheeks turned a light shade of pink. "It really doesn't suit you." She set in in the nightstand and slid the drawer closed. "I do appreciate your concern but I'm okay. My brother and I are, well, let's just say we're on opposite sides of the law. I've tried for years to get him to straighten out but I don't think he knows any other way to be."

"That happens more often than you'd think with siblings. Is he okay?"

Dixie was almost in tears and she let out a nervous laugh. "For him? Yeah, he's okay. When I saw him today, his face was all bruised up, he was dirty, and he didn't have any shoes."

Her last statement was so matter of fact that Rock waited for her to continue. When she didn't, he stood up and looked at her. "Is there anything I can do for you? I'm guessing he probably calls you whenever he's in some sort of trouble. Are you sure you're safe?"

"I'm good. Like I said, I turned my phone off..." at that thought, she reached into her pocket and pulled it out so she could turn it back on.

"And I made sure no one was following me when I was on my way home. I even took a few detours just to be safe."

Rock nodded. "Call me if you need anything. I'm sorry again about... all this." He gestured around the room as if she didn't know what he was talking about.

"Lucky for me, you already knew my secrets." She stood and walked him to the door. She held it open for him. "Thank you for stopping by to check on me." She smiled at him and watched him walk to his car before locking the door behind him.

A single tear made its way down her face as she walked into the bedroom and laid down on her bed. She could never hate her brother for what he did but sometimes she hated what he put her through. She knew it was dangerous for her to stick around as long as she did today but she was terrified to walk away, as always, worried it would be the last time she saw him. Having known Rock for only a few weeks, she was overwhelmed by the idea that he was worried enough about her to check in on her. That would never have happened at her old station and she had been there for years.

The main wall was covered with a woodland scene of pastel, baby animals. In the center was an image of a spotted fawn. Rock noticed a glare on the wall and saw a spotlight runner attached to the ceiling with one light perfectly aimed at the wall. He liked the idea of not having the child's name in the room but rather a character depicting it. The image of the baby deer was a perfect substitute for the name Fawn. He ran his eyes over the image to see if there were any other hidden messages held within. As his eyes neared the ceiling, he spotted the dark colored cow that looked like it was leaping through the air. "The cow jumped over the moon."

Dixie looked at him with her eyes narrowed and then followed his gaze. She saw exactly what he was looking at. "Someone hit the light switch for me?" The room darkened and a perfectly lit quarter moon shape appeared on the wall. "Thank you. You can turn them back on." She turned to look at Rock. "Well, you were right. The cow is jumping over the moon." She took a few steps forward and then looked up at the light. A single sheet of paper was attached to the light bulb, covering all but the edge of one side. "Oh. Do you think with this setup it means our person has been here before? I mean, if nothing else, they would have to know this runner exists, right?"

Rock pondered the idea for a moment before agreeing. "They would. Not because of the woodland scene, uh, even though the cow doesn't fit, but because they would have to know they were able to make it project like that on the wall. It wouldn't work if there was just an overhead light like there are in most apartments."

"Let's go find out who has been here since she put that up."

Stephanie was sitting at the kitchen table when Dixie walked in. The counter was covered with more small appliances than she had ever seen in one house. The island that separated the room from the living area was loaded with boxes of food. Dixie took note that they were all branded with labels showing they were organic, fair trade, or GMO free. She joined Stephanie at the table and went through the basic questions. She was the most cooperative Dixie had come across so far and she was thankful to finally have someone that understood the importance of her questions.

Dixie thought she could almost answer the questions from memory now since everyone seemed to have almost the exact same answers in one form or another. She was shocked when Stephanie had a different answer to one of those questions. She told her she did have someone she didn't know give Fawn an unusual amount of attention just two days before. She looked over and saw her partner talking to Gemini in the living room. "Hey, Rock. Come have a seat." She pulled out the chair next to her while he made his way over. "Thought you might want to hear this part." She nodded toward Stephanie for her to continue.

"Two days ago, I had to run to the post office and pick up some fresh vegetables. It was beautiful outside so I decided it would be nice to take Fawn for a walk before running the errands. I stopped at Sol Smoothie, it's a little out of the way but it's all natural ingredients. Anyway, I ordered my drink and the lady that was in line behind me started up a conversation. A lot of people do, they lose their minds whenever a baby is around, but she kept sticking her face in the stroller and I didn't like that very much. I had to ask her twice to back away from Fawn. Don't get me wrong, she was nice enough during the conversation but it's in poor taste to get that close to a baby you don't know."

Dixie and Rock nodded. "Was there anything else that made you uncomfortable about her or made her stand out to you?"

"Mhm. She was dressed way too warm for the weather. It was early morning so it was still a little cooler out but she was dressed like it was winter. It almost looked like she was homeless and was wearing all her possessions so no one stole them. But you can't be homeless and afford to be able to buy a smoothie from Sol."

Rock leaned over Dixie to see what she had written in her notebook so far. "Have you seen any of the press releases we've done or read any of the articles about infants being taken in the city over the last few weeks?"

Stephanie dropped her eyes to the table. "No. I try not to watch the news or read it. I live in the city, there's always so much bad news that I actively try to avoid it. I grew up in a small town where nothing newsworthy ever happened. When I moved to the city, I realized I couldn't mentally handle all the bad stuff that happened on a daily basis, so I stopped looking at it." They could both see the anguish in her eyes. "Do you think I could have stopped this from happening to Fawn?" As soon as the words escaped her mouth, tears flowed down her cheeks.

Rock gently touched the top of her hand. "You couldn't have prevented it. The press releases were put out to caution people and to ask for any information people may have. Since our first release, we've only had a hand full of calls and most of them, like always, were just people looking for attention.

She nodded her head just enough for them to notice. Rock knew she was having trouble believing it wasn't her fault. She was only the third to show any sign of regret for what had happened, at least while they were still present.

At the station, Rock pinned the new location to the board and added the bingo ball number. He drew an "X" over the smoothie shop that they would be visiting shortly. The shop was located outside the area they had marked with pins. He tapped on the board to get Dixie's attention. "What do you think? You think this is enough to say this person is purposely following our victims?"

"We do have two people who have seen her so far. At least, I'm guessing it's the same person. They both described her style of dress the same way. And it's too much of a coincidence for both of them to have had a casual conversation with her. The park and the smoothie shop are nowhere near each other."

"All right. Let's go interview the shop employees and we'll see if we have any camera footage from nearby businesses. This is a nicer area than our center location here. Maybe we'll have better luck."

Dixie rolled her eyes to the ceiling. "I think you have a more positive outlook than I do but let's check it out."

Dixie hadn't been to this side of town yet with the exception of going to Stephanie's last night. Rock was right about this being a much nicer area than the other. Aside from the smoothie shop, there was also an upscale boutique, a gift shop, a cupcake shop, and a yoga studio. Rock asked to speak to the manager when they walked into the shop and they both flashed their badges. Her name tag read "Brittany" and her appearance screamed 'health food junkie'. Her curls bounced as she walked and her smile was wider than her face.

"What can I do for you?" her voice was so high pitched Dixie cringed when she began to speak.

Rock shook his head quickly to each side in an attempt to rid it of the piercing sound that had just ripped through it. "We're hoping you'll be able to tell us who was working two days ago, around eight thirty."

"Sure. I was here."

"Great." Rock forced a smile across his face but didn't try to hide the disappointment in his voice.

"Joanna and Milo were also here." She pointed out the two workers standing behind the counter.

The amount of energy she had at seven in the morning was exhausting. "We wanted to ask about a woman that was here that morning. Unfortunately, we don't have much information to give about her, which is why we're here."

"I can try to help. I know almost all of our customers by name. It's essential to making them feel important."

"Uh, huh. Like I said, we don't have much. The main description we have of her is that she was wearing clothing too warm for the weather and she had on a lot of scarves."

Milo bounced over to where they were standing and leaned over the counter. "Pashmina."

"I'm sorry?"

"The scarves she was wearing were pashmina. They're super expensive but if you can find one at a reasonable price, oh, it's like having heaven itself wrapped around you." He hugged himself and closed his eyes as if he could feel the material on his skin.

"Really? The common assumption on first meeting her seemed to be that she gave off the impression of being homeless."

"Well, she's certainly no fashionista, if that's what you're asking, but she's not homeless."

"Do you know the woman? Can you give us her name?" Rock's eyes were wide and hopeful.

"Oh, I wish I could help. That was the first time I ever saw her. Plus, I don't think she liked me very much. She was having a whole conversation with some other woman in line but when I tried to talk to her, she was very short with me. As soon as I handed her her drink, she all but ran out the door. Just this side of rude, if you ask me."

Dixie could see Rock's shoulders sag. "Are you sure you've never seen her before? Maybe she looked a little different? Less scarves or something?"

"I would have remembered. Your homeless comment makes sense and she doesn't exactly fit in with the rest of our clientele. Take a look at the people here now. They're all conscious of what they look like and how they carry themselves. This woman you're asking about is, well, frumpy." He threw his hands to the side to indicate that he was done speaking.

"Okay. Thank you for your time." Rock passed Milo a business card. "If she happens to come in again, please, give us a call right away."

"Ooh." He flipped the card over in his hand a few times. "Am I like, a police spy now?"

"No." Rock watched as the pout spread across his face. "You're someone who could help us with an important case if you call us without alerting her."

"Okay." The frown was frozen on his face while he slid the card into the back pocket of his skinny jeans.

Dixie laughed when they walked out the door. "Wow, Rock. You just ruined his entire day."

He looked at her with his eyebrows raised. "A police spy? Really?"

"Oh, but he was so excited about it."

"I'm already regretting giving him my card. Next thing I know, he'll be calling my phone at four a.m. to tell me about someone he saw at a hotdog stand three years ago that may have been her."

They had to wait nearly three hours for the other businesses on the block to open so they swung by the lab to pick up the pictures of the new crime scene.

"You know, if it wasn't for the circumstances, that moon and cow thing would actually be kind of pretty. It's a cool concept." Leave it to Gemini to find the one beautiful thing in a crime scene. "Of course, you'd have to remove that cute woodland background."

Rock blinked at her slowly while she spoke. "You didn't sleep much either, huh?"

"Not a wink. I had just laid down when I got the call." She held up one finger and walked into another room. She returned with an evidence bag in her hand. "I do have some good news. At least, I hope it'll prove to be good news." She looked at Dixie who had down turned lips and a furrowed brow. "Are you okay?"

She remained silent for a moment. "Do you have a bathroom I could use?"

Gemini dug into her pocket and pulled out a key card. "Down the hall to the right." She pointed and handed Dixie the card. "This will get you in there and back in here."

"Thanks." She left the room without another word.

"Anyway, I hope it'll be a good thing. This case is just about killing all of us. If I didn't know better I would swear it was a cop or someone in the forensics field because of the lack of evidence." She held up the bag and Rock took it from her. "We found a hair stuck to the tape that was holding the light covering in place. And, it has a follicle attached. No promises, as you know, but even if we don't find a match in the system, at least we have something to go on. Something to compare future evidence against."

"Best news I could have heard all day. Hey, do you know what a pas, pasha, pasmin, uh." He pulled his notebook from his pocket and flipped it open. "Pashmina? Do you know what a pashmina scarf is?"

Her eyes widened. "Yes, I know what it is. It's like having a weightless chinchilla hugging your neck. It's not chinchilla, it's actually a very fine goat hair but just as soft. Why?"

"Is that something you would be able to test for if you were to find it?"

Gemini pursed her lips and then sighed. "If it wasn't you asking, Rock, I'd be completely offended by that question."

"Sorry. I don't even know why I asked. I don't know if it's a potential lead or not but if you could have your guys keep an eye out."

"It would be unlikely to be found but I'll let them know."

They both turned when they heard the click of the door from the key card. Dixie handed the card back to Gemini and thanked her.

"Let me know when you get the results from that hair?"

"You got it. I'll call you either way."

They had barely made it out to the car when Dixie received a text from Gemini asking again if she was okay. She replied back and pushed her phone back into her pocket.

It was nearing lunch by the time they made it back to the station. Of all the shops on the block, only one had a video camera and it didn't show any part of the street. The owner allowed them to watch the video feed from the days prior but it proved useless. She was also clear about her stance that if any person walked into her store and looked as though they may be homeless, she wouldn't have allowed them to stay. Rock needed only to look at two tags with triple digit prices to know she wasn't joking.

He was leaning back in his chair with his hands covering his face and his feet, crossed at the ankles, on the top of his desk. "We should call a meeting. We'll make a list of places: churches, grocery stores, coffee shops, parks. Let's get the women down here to see if any of the places they frequent are the same. Maybe we'll get really lucky and a few of them will know each other, at least by sight if nothing else."

"That's a great idea. I'll start calling if you make a list of places to ask about. When do you want them here?"

"Let's give them a little time. Nine tomorrow morning?"

"You got it." Dixie reached over and wiggled the mouse to bring her computer screen to life. "Should we call Morgan in just for fun?" Her grin was wicked.

Rock's eyes narrowed. "Do you want help solving the case or would you prefer to bail me out of jail?"

Dixie opened her mouth to reply and then thought better of it.

"Good decision."

Dixie wrote down the names and phone numbers of the women and started calling. "You know, I'm really not looking forward to having all these women together in one room. They're bad enough one on one."

"Hmm. If it doesn't work out, we'll start our own cat fighting ring. We can split the profits."

The following morning, Dixie could barely hear herself think. She gazed through the window of the meeting room at the eclectic group of women standing around the table. They hadn't stopped talking since they walked in. There was a five to three ratio of those wearing yoga pants versus those who weren't and there was enough makeup in the room to fully make over an entire circus team, clowns included.

Rock was purposely fidgeting around with stuff on his desk, making the women wait. He wanted to give them some time to see if any of them recognized each other. When he walked into the room, all the women stopped talking and stared at him.

Dixie chuckled quietly behind his back assuming it was the first time any of them had actually looked at him as a man rather than a detective. Three of the women had their mouths hanging open and the rest were deer in headlights. "Ladies. Thank you all for coming in today and for being so cooperative on such short notice. We're going to try to keep this as brief as possible. If you could all take a seat." He waited for the scratching of chairs to stop before continuing. "I know you have all been in here chatting for a few minutes but the first thing I'd like you to do is take a look around the table and let us know if you recognize anyone else here outside of your meeting today. Think hard about it. Maybe you had a brief conversation somewhere?"

There were a few grumblings among them but no one could place any of the other women.

"Okay. We're going to go around the table a number of times. I'm going to name a general place and I need you to tell me specifically which places you frequent so we can try to find some connection between all of you."

Brenda rolled her eyes. "You couldn't have just asked us over the phone? It would have saved us all a bunch of time."

"You're right. But the hope is that maybe if you hear the name of some other place, it may trigger your memory on having gone there once or twice. Does anyone have any questions before we start?"

The women shook their heads, some sat there with a blank stare on their faces.

"All right. We're going to start with Charlotte and work our way around the table. I name the place, you tell me all the places you frequent." Rock went through his list asking for grocery stores, churches, clothing stores, gyms, smoothie shops, dry cleaners.

Brenda piped up again when he asked about the dry cleaners. "Take a look around detective. Do you honestly think the majority of us can afford to go to the dry cleaner? Come on."

"I'm not asking if you can afford it. A lot of people can afford it and still choose not to do it. If you don't have one, just say you don't have one and we'll move on." He went through a few more before landing on coffee shops.

"Brew Masters."

"Albert's."

"From the Grind Up."

"Mocha Raton."

"Ooh. I've been there a few times when I was in the neighborhood."

"Good. Anyone else? Mocha Raton?"

"I went once when they first opened but that was a few years ago. I haven't been back since."

Rock nodded at Siobhan to continue.

"Mochaschino Cherie." She said it with an uppity accent that caused the other women to turn and stare at her. "What? It's how it's pronounced. It's a cute little coffee house over on MontClair. They have a regular shop that's open in the morning and then a back room that opens at night. The night options are a little more expensive but you can have a s'mores bar brought right to your table. It's a great place if you're not into bars and nightclubs."

"Can you not pronounce it like the rest of us would have? That pretentious accent was a little much."

"Well. It's not my fault some of us can actually afford dry cleaners."

"I can afford it and you still sound ridiculous."

"Either way, we're all still sitting in the same room now and our financial status hasn't helped any of us with this."

Dixie looked at Melinda in shock. She wasn't aware she knew how to stand up for herself.

"Ladies, that's enough. Melinda is right. This has nothing to do with money. Let's move on."

When they were through with the list of twenty-seven places, he passed a piece of paper and a pen to each woman and asked her to write down the list of doctors she saw for any reason.

"Do I have to write down every doctor I see at Northwestern? I have quite a few because of some issues I had while I was pregnant."

Dixie started to speak but was interrupted by all the ladies speaking in unison.

"Hold on, quiet." Rock's voice cut through the room and it went silent. "Raise your hand if you gave birth at Northwestern." Every hand in the room went up.

Brenda had a smug look on her face. "I told you you could have just called us." Her chair squealed against the cement floor as she stood to leave.

"We don't know for sure that's the connection but it gives us a place to look. Please, finish writing your list of medical providers and hand them to us on your way out. Thank you all for taking the time to come see us today."

Dixie and Rock whispered among themselves while the women were finishing their lists and said goodbye as they all got up to leave.

"The hospital is so obvious."

Rock nodded. "Probably why we never thought of it. I was focused on where they lived."

"Let's start our list and see if they had the same OB-GYN or labor and delivery nurse. Maybe we'll finally get lucky."

Rock pulled a second white board from a meeting room and began listing doctor's and nurses' names that were mentioned from the hospital. After a full hour of comparing the lists from all eight women, they had a full board and no definitive matches. "This doesn't help much. The most we have is a Dr. Whittaker that is common among four of them. Dr. Sampson has two and Dr. Nowakowski has two."

"What about the nurses? They usually work in rotating shifts, right? Maybe we can find a nurse or two that was present during each birth, we'd just need to find out what time of day each baby was born and compare it with the shifts the nurses were working."

"It's not quite that easy. When Ella was born, I saw a different nurse every time I was there. It's a place to start though. Maybe it'll be the other obvious piece that we're missing."

When they arrived at the hospital, they were greeted by the same woman who had helped them the first time. "Detectives. What brings you in this time?"

"We were hoping to speak to a couple of the doctors if they're here today. This hospital seems to be a common thread in our investigation."

"As I'm sure you're aware, the doctors are extremely busy. Perhaps it would be best to call and set up an appointment with them?"

Dixie almost laughed. "You and I both know that's not an option. We do need to speak to them as soon as possible, not just sometime this year. So, if you could kindly tell us which of these doctors are here right now, we'd appreciate it." The tone in her voice had changed and the nurse took the list from her hand.

She looked it over. "Dr. Whittaker is here now. Doctors Nowakowski and Sampson should be here soon. Shifts are about to change."

"That's better. Could you page Dr. Whittaker, please?"

They stood in the waiting room for nearly twenty minutes before the doctor came out to greet them.

"Detectives. Walk with me. I'm very busy." He never slowed his pace as he made his way through the room.

Rock was able to step in line with him but Dixie had to run a little to catch up. Dr. Whittaker, I presume? I'm Detective Rockefe..."

"I don't have time for introductions. Just leave your card. What can I do for you?"

Rock rolled his eyes before continuing. "As I'm sure you're aware, there has been a string of abductions involving infants."

Dr. Whittaker stopped abruptly and turned to look at them. "I don't need ten years' worth of back story. I'm busy. Please, just tell me what you need." He turned and resumed walking down the dimly lit corridor.

While the doctor was facing them, Dixie caught a glimpse of his name tag. *Harold Whittaker: Chief Physician*. She also noticed how heavy his hair sat on his head. It was more salt than pepper but she had a suspicion it was a toupee. It was so perfectly aligned, she imagined if one strand moved, the rest would move with it. He had a strong build that matched his personality and she thought, in his prime, he was probably considered a good looking man. Now, after years of working under what was sure to be an enormous amount of stress, dark circles hung under his eyes and deep lines tunneled through his skin.

"Fine. All the victims are linked to your hospital. We need an interview with you, two of your fellow doctors, and all of your nursing staff."

The doctor hesitated just enough so it looked like he skipped a step and bluntly responded, "No."

Dixie stepped in then as one of her pet peeves is people saying "no." "Dr. Whittaker, given your position here in the hospital, I have to reason that you're a rather intelligent man. I'm sure we don't need to tell you that it wasn't an option and we weren't asking."

Rock nodded his head at her in approval. He had heard her get snippy with a few people since they started working together but her tone here was different. It commanded respect and he liked that.

The doctor had finally stopped walking and was now facing them, glaring. His shoulders sagged but his face was like stone. "I'll have Marianne send the nurses in to meet you one at a time. You can use our small conference room. As for the doctors, you can figure that out yourselves. I'll stop by the station on my way in tomorrow." He put out his hand and Rock fished a business card out of his jacket pocket.

It took almost four hours between the times the first nurse came in until they called for the last. They were both exhausted. The conference room was warm and stuffy. Both of them had had to take a few breaks between nurses to walk into the hallway to catch their breath and clear their heads.

"How many do we have left?" Rock's face was beaded with sweat and he looked like he could fall asleep at any moment.

"Just one... a Shaina Martin." Seeing the look of dread on Rock's face she added, "On the bright side, this is the very last one. We came on a good day and got to speak to them all."

There was a knock on the door and a petite brunette poked her head in. "I heard you wanted to talk to me?"

Dixie looked over to her and smiled. "You must be Shaina. Come on in." She gestured to the empty chair resting against the wall.

Shaina had a mousy appearance with a high-pitched, squeaky voice to match it.

"We won't keep you long. We just have a few questions and then you can get back to work."

The following morning, they were both leaning back in their chairs, defeated. The nurses were of little help. They were all willing to point fingers but no one had any real information, they mostly just reiterated what they had seen on the news and expressed concern for the mothers involved and well wishes for the infants. The general consensus was that they all liked Doctors Nowakowski and Sampson but could take or leave Dr. Whittaker, not for any reason other than his personality flaws. According to the nurses, he spent little time with the mothers or infants and the majority of his time was spend holed up in his office. No one knew what he did while he was in there.

As promised, he stopped by first thing and was less than forthcoming. It was no wonder to Dixie and Rock why the nurses and other doctors didn't have much to say about him. He did come prepared with documents showing his schedule and hours worked. After another quick visit to the hospital to verify, they were able to cross him off the list of potential suspects, putting them back to zero.

Even though it was early, Rock decided to hit the club on his way home. None of the regular dancers were there but he didn't care, he wasn't really paying much attention. He just wanted to enjoy a drink and decompress without risking the possibility of running into anyone he knew from work. He was just finishing his first glass of whiskey when his phone buzzed. "Every time," he moaned louder than he intended. He pulled it from his pocket and saw Jill's name flashing on the screen. "Shit." He half ran outside to get away from the volume of the music.

"Hello." He listened to her hysterics for a solid minute before he could get a word in. "Where are you now?" He put her on speaker and sent a text to Stone while she was still talking. "Stay there. We'll be there soon." He hung up just in time for Stone to call him.

"Hey Captain." He ran to his car while he was talking. "She locked herself in the bathroom at O'Brien's' deli. I'm heading over there now."

Chapter IX

They peered over the window ledge, watching Rock's wife feed their baby. Such a good mother. It's a shame that baby will soon disappear.

Rock ran in to the deli and was ushered to the bathroom by a patrol officer that stopped when he heard the call.

"I was only a block away when I heard the call come through. I've tried to get her to come out but she refused. Said she'd only open the door when you got here."

"Thank you." They were the only words Rock could get out. He knocked on the door quietly so he didn't scare Jill any more than she already was. "Jill? It's me. Can you open the door, please?"

The door hinge squeaked as it opened just wide enough for her to peer through the crack. "Oh, Larry." The door swung open and she threw herself into his arms.

Rock wrapped his arms around her and held her tight. He could feel her trembling. "Tell me what happened."

She eased her grasp and backed away from him. "I was at the little market around the corner. I don't usually go out this late but I wasn't sure we had enough milk for coffee in the morning. It was still warm out so I decided to take Ella for a walk instead of going to the convenience store that I would normally go to. All I did was lean down to reach into the cooler. It was five seconds, I swear." She looked at him, her eyes pleading. "When I stood up, she had both of her hands on Ella. Like she was going to pick her up and run. I screamed as loud as I could and I think I startled her. She took her hands out of the stroller and stood up and stared at me." Her eyes were beginning to water and her voice was breaking up. "I grabbed the stroller and ran over here as fast as I could. It was the only place I could think of where I could lock myself in."

Rock leaned in and hugged her again. "You did great, Jill. That's exactly what you should have done."

Stone arrived but hadn't said a word. He simply shook his head at Rock to let him know they hadn't found the woman they were looking for.

The patrol officer who was the first to arrive on the scene had made his way around Jill and Rock to check on Ella. When he saw Stone, he motioned him into the bathroom. He leaned over to the stroller the officer was crouched in front of to see what he was looking at. Wrapped around the front tire, having been dragged almost a block, was a thin blue scarf.

A permanent detail was put on Rock's house. There were two officers assigned to keep watch even when he was home. He was still hesitant to leave in the morning but he had to go to the station. He spoke to each officer before he left to make sure they had his personal number so they could call him immediately if they saw anything suspicious.

He wasn't at the station five minutes before Richard came storming through the door demanding Chrissy be arrested for breaking her restraining order.

"Hold on. Take a seat, settle down a bit."

Richard sat down and took a deep breath. "I want Chrissy arrested. She showed up at my job this morning, screaming, accusing me of taking Charlotte. I told her to leave but she wouldn't."

"Have you spoken to her at all since Charlotte left? You won't be in trouble if you reached out to her, but we need to know the truth."

"No. I told you before, I don't want anything to do with either one of them."

"Did she say why she was there? Was there a reason she showed up after this long?"

"She was hysterical. I could barely understand what she saying. She was waving this piece of paper in my face and she crumpled it up and threw it at me." He reached into his pocket to pull it out and handed it to Dixie. "I didn't even read it."

Dixie did her best to uncrumple the ball he had placed in her hand. She read the words out loud. "Are you sure you trust Richard didn't have a hand in taking Charlotte?"

"I swear. I didn't touch the kid. I've never even seen her."

"We'll need a statement from you before you leave. We'll take care of Chrissy."

They left him in the hands of another detective and drove over to Chrissy's apartment. "This is such bullshit. I can't believe we have to arrest a victim." He shook his head as he spoke.

"I just don't understand what she was thinking. Why wouldn't she just come to us and tell us about the note?"

"I have no idea. She's not the sharpest tack."

They knocked on her door and she answered it without taking the time to see who it was first. She opened it wide enough for them to walk in but they remained in the hallway.

"We heard you went to see Richard this morning."

"Yes, I did. He knows where she is. He has to."

"He doesn't. And you broke your restraining order."

Her mouth hung open while she processed Dixie's last response. "You're kidding? You're seriously going to arrest me for this?"

"I'm afraid so. You had options, you could have come to us with the note and asked us to talk to him again. You know you're not allowed to contact him for any reason."

Chrissy sighed and stepped into the hallway, closing the door behind her. "Fine."

By the time they had left the station, Leila had already published an evening article bashing them for arresting a victim of an ongoing case. It wasn't a surprise to any of them. They all hated the situation but if they didn't arrest Chrissy, another officer would have. It didn't put them in a good light but nothing about this case was helping with that.

Over the next three weeks, the calls continued to come in right on time. The list of rhymes was growing, the bingo balls kept rolling. Nothing was bringing them any closer to finding the kidnapper and Rock was beginning to lose his focus. He was thinking about his wife and daughter while at work and work while at home. Over the last week he had considered numerous times telling Stone he couldn't handle the case any longer.

Dixie called Steve on her way home, hoping he would be available. "It's me. Want to come help me celebrate?"

"Always. What are we celebrating?"

"How about the fact that I'm not pregnant?"

"Now that *is* something to celebrate. Give me an hour."

It took him less than forty-five minutes to meet her. He had just finished fastening her second ankle to the bed when the front door burst open. Dixie jumped and felt the pull in her limbs.

He narrowed his eyes and looked at her laying before him. "Are you expecting company?" He could see her straining to hear.

"No."

He moved stealthily to the door and peered down the hallway.

"Dixie? Are you home?" Branden's voice carried into the bedroom.

"Shit. It's my brother."

Steve turned to look at her, a smile crept across his face and he walked back over to the bed. "Call him in here."

Dixie's jaw dropped. She was sprawled in the middle of her bed wearing nothing more than black, lace undergarments. "You're kidding, right? It's my brother!"

He wrapped his hand under her chin before leaning down and kissing her lips. "Now is not the time you want to disobey me. Call him in."

The tone of his voice told her this wasn't part of their agreement and she should do as he asked. She heard the refrigerator door close and a can of soda pop open.

"Dixie?"

"In the bedroom." She tried to keep her voice as even as possible but her nerves were getting the best of her. This was the first time, after knowing Steve for years, she had ever been uncomfortable in his presence.

Branden all but sprinted into the bedroom before coming to a halt and shielding his eyes. "You could have warned me." He turned to leave but the words coming from the other side of the door stopped him.

"It's been a long time, Branden."

His breathing sped up and he spun around on the ball of his foot. His eyes were wide. "Please don't hurt my sister, she didn't know I'd be here."

"Oh," his smile was wide and deliberate. "I'd never hurt Dixie unless she asked real nice. It's part of our deal. But, I wouldn't do anything stupid if I were you."

Branden looked back and forth between Dixie and Steve. "What deal?"

Dixie had sunk into the bed as far as she could go. She had no idea what was happening. "Do you two know each other?"

"Why don't you go take a seat next to her and explain how we're acquainted?"

He took one step forward and hesitated. "She's practically naked."

"That wasn't a question."

Reluctant, he made his way to the bed and sat as far on the edge as he could without sliding off. Keeping his eyes on the wall in front of him, he explained to Dixie that her friend was one of the men that had been hunting him for the past few years. "He's one of the best. And the most dangerous. He's able to find me whether I'm in town or three states away." His voice faded as he finished the last few words. "Oh, my god! You're sleeping with a guy that's trying to kill me."

Dixie could only see the side of his face but she saw the look of betrayal it carried and her chest constricted. "Branden, I didn't know." She felt like she was going to be sick. The one man she had trusted most in her life, even more than her work partners, had betrayed her in the worst possible way. In an instant, all of her hurt turned to anger. "You son of a bitch." She spat the words at him before remembering her compromising position. The handcuffs tore into her wrists and the post of her headboard fractured under the pressure of her movement. "I trusted you."

He tilted his head and a pitiful look set into his eyes. "And you should continue to do so. Do you really think your brother being able to escape every time someone found him was just dumb luck? I'm good at what I do, Dixie." He ran his eyes down the length of her body, "everything that I do. I've been protecting Branden since the day I met you."

Dixie's entire body was tense, her face red with anger. "He just said you've been trying to kill him."

"I'm a P.I., I don't kill people. I carry a gun for my own protection."

"Then why are you following him?"

Steve shook his head, annoyed that she wasn't catching on. "The only way I can protect him is by knowing where he is. The people looking for him pay me, very well I might add, to find him. So, I find him, and then I follow him to make sure they don't kill him."

"Oh, yeah? Where were you a week ago when they jumped him? They took all his stuff, they beat him. He had to give his shoes to a homeless guy just so he could call me. So much for protection."

He was beginning to get angry now. "I think you're missing the point here. Branden wouldn't have survived the first encounter if it wasn't for me, never mind every one after that. Do you have any idea how many chances they've had to kill him? Let's face it, Dixie, his survival instincts aren't exactly the best. He knowingly puts himself in this position."

"But you lead them right to him."

"Yes, because if I don't, they'll find someone else who will."

Branden cleared his throat to remind them that he was still in the room. He looked so young with his eyes wide and mouth set in a frown, like a child caught in the middle of his parent's argument.

Dixie took one look at him and turned back on Steve. "Get out of my house." Her teeth were clenched and she forced the words through them.

Steve turned to leave but stopped in the doorway. "Branden, get your shit together. If not for yourself, do it for your sister because I won't always be there to protect you." He turned half-way and then back again. "And Dixie, for what it's worth, the reason I took this assignment, the main reason he's still alive? It's because I'm in love with you." He pulled the handcuff keys from his pocket and tossed them to the bed. "You know how to find me."

Dixie let Branden spend the night at her house. She couldn't bring herself to ask him to leave again. She laid in bed staring at her ceiling all night, waiting and listening for any sign that someone was outside. She drifted off for less than an hour before her alarm woke her and Branden was gone when she walked out of her bedroom.

She was having trouble coming to terms with what Steve had revealed the previous evening and she couldn't decide if she wanted him to keep looking out for Branden or not. She wanted to trust him to keep her brother safe but she wasn't sure she could trust him at all anymore.

Rock was already at the station when she walked in. "Good morning."

"I guess. You okay?"

"Not really. But I don't want to talk about it. I just had a long night."

"Well, don't get too comfortable. I got a note this morning."

"Oh? What did it say?"

"It told me to find Shaina because she has information that I want." He waited for what he said to register.

"Shaina? That little, mousey nurse? What could she possibly know?"

"The note didn't have a last name but she's the only Shaina we've met so far. Let's go find out."

The waiting room was almost empty and Marianne was sitting at the desk with her face buried in her phone.

"Quiet day?"

She looked up, startled, at the sound of Rock's voice. "Good morning, detectives. Yes, it's been unusually quiet so far."

"Lucky for us. We need to speak to Shaina Martin. Is she here today?"

Her head was already shaking from side to side. "Sorry, no. Shaina called out sick today."

"Does she call out often?" Dixie tried to keep her tone inquisitive rather than accusatory but Marianne didn't seem to buy it by the look on her face.

"No, she doesn't. But I spoke to her myself. She doesn't sound very good."

Dixie flipped open her notebook. "Do you have a home address for her?"

Marianne eyes rolled up toward the ceiling. "Please don't make me remind you that I can't give out that information."

She flicked her wrist up, closing her notebook and slipped it back into her pocket. "Okay. We'll look it up ourselves. Wouldn't want you to trouble yourself."

"It's no trouble for me. I'm just not allowed to give it out."

They had just started for the exit when the swinging, double doors burst open and Dr. Sampson and Shaina came walking into the waiting room.

Rock turned and glared at Marianne. "I thought you said Shaina wasn't here?"

The small, mousey girl stopped so fast her sneakers squeaked on the tiled floor.

"That's not Shaina." Her eyes were narrowed and darted back and forth between the nurse and the detectives. "That's Kelly. She's an intern."

Rock walked over to her and leaned down so he was no more than an inch from her face. "You can explain now or you can come down to the station with us and explain it there."

Kelly stumbled back a step, her mouth fell open, and she looked up at Dr. Sampson, her eyes pleading with him to help her. "She told me I had to." Her gaze shifted to the floor and she moved her foot back and forth like she was stubbing out a cigarette with the toe of her shoe.

Rock straightened up and addressed Dr. Sampson. "Is that conference room open?"

Dr. Sampson nodded and gestured to the hall where the room was located.

Dixie put her hand on Kelly's back between her shoulder blades and prompted her to follow Rock down the hall. They could hear the mumblings of (nurse) and Dr. Sampson as they walked away.

Rock held the door open for Kelly and Dixie and slammed it shut once they entered.

Kelly jumped and let out an involuntary squeal of terror.

Dixie guided her to a chair and Rock sat on the table to face her.

"She told you you had to? Are you not capable of thinking or acting on your own?"

"I am. But, I'm only an intern. She told me I had to get used to talking to the police."

"We checked your badge when you came in to talk to us. How did you get one with her name on it?"

"She gave it to me. I guess she has some kind of access to security that I don't have."

"Uh, huh. So, you just went along with it? You didn't ask any questions?"

"I did. I asked her why I had to do it. She told me I had to get used to talking to you guys. She also said she had a little bit of a history with you and she didn't want to face you just yet. Shaina has been very good to me since I've been working here. I was uncomfortable pretending to be her but I didn't think she would steer me in the wrong direction."

"What kind of history does she have with us?"

"I...I don't know. I didn't ask her.

"How long have you been an intern here?"

"A few months."

"Could you be a little more specific? Ah, keeping in mind that we can arrest you right now for obstruction?"

Kelly's eyes widened. "What? How?"

"How long have you been here?" Dixie was leaning over Kelly's shoulder, her words sharp in her ear.

"I've been here a little over three months. I started right before the babies started getting kidnapped."

"That's better." Rock relaxed his shoulders and slid off the table into a chair. "How much do you know about Shaina? Do you know where she lives?"

"I don't know much about her. I've tried to get to know her but she likes to keep to herself. I don't actually know where she lives. She's only said she lives on the south side of the city but she's been spending a lot of time at her brother's house."

"Did she say why?"

Kelly shook her head. "Only that it was closer. She doesn't like driving all the way home if she works after dark."

"Do you know where he lives? His name? Anything about him?"

She shrugged and shook her head. "I told you, she doesn't say much."

They spent the rest of the morning and afternoon trying to track Shaina down. They couldn't find any bills in her name, no mortgage loans, no car payments. It was like she was a ghost. They got a signed warrant for the hospital to release her address but it proved useless. After driving almost an hour to the address, they were met with a condemned building on the south side of the city. It's boarded up windows were covered in graffiti and the building was beginning to lean to the side. It had clearly been unoccupied for years.

Feeling defeated once again, they went back to the station before going home to rest for a few hours. Their next call would be coming in soon.

Chapter X

All of this could have been prevented.

They all met at the station at eleven at the request of Stone. Rock and Dixie were the first to arrive, Henry showed up next. Stone and Gemini walked through the door engaged in conversation and the forensics team filtered in over the next twenty minutes. It would be day number four soon and they wanted to be together when the next call came in. Rock had requested a detail for his wife and they set her up in a hotel with an officer stationed outside her room.

They spent the first couple hours talking and milling about, staring at the white board, trying to make sense of a pattern that wasn't there. Around one o'clock, they all settled down and silently watched the minutes tick by, waiting for the phone to ring, secretly hoping it didn't. Hours drifted by and they were all looking for something to themselves occupied and awake. They'd become numb to the sound of the air conditioner buzzing overhead, the tapping of pens on desktops, the shuffling of paper.

At four-thirty the station door opened and a young man entered. A baseball cap all but covered his eyes and his hood was pulled up over his head. Everyone turned and stared. His jaw slackened and he stood motionless.

Gemini was the only one who thought to say anything to their guest. "Can we help you?"

He blinked a few times before responding, having been caught off guard by all the attention. "I'm looking for," he looked down at the manila envelope in his hand, "Detective Rockefeller."

Rock stepped forward and put his hand out to take the envelope. "Where'd you get this from?"

The young man shrugged. "Some guy gave me fifty bucks to bring this over here and give it to you. I wasn't gonna say no. I was going this way anyway."

"Where were you headed so early?"

"I'm going to work."

"You're going to be late." Rock glanced over his shoulder. "Someone get some information this kid."

Gemini removed her hand from Rock's shoulder and eased the envelope out of his hand. She used a letter opener she had found in a desk drawer and carefully slit the top open. She tilted the envelope toward the desk and dumped the contents.

Dixie leaned around Gemini to see what was there. She reached her arm around and grabbed the bingo card that sat on top of the pile, running it over to the white board.

"Son of a bitch!" All the color drained from Rock's face and Gemini eased him into a nearby chair.

"Stone. We need every available squad car at the hotel. Now!" The picture of the front of the hotel where they had sent Jill was a figurative knife through the hearts of all those who could see it.

"Someone get me a pencil. And a marker." Dixie shouted as her eyes darted back and forth between the bingo card and the map where they had been placing the numbers.

The station, which had been nearly silent ten minutes before, was now complete chaos. People were running back and forth, shouting to each other and into phones, slamming desk drawers.

Dixie busied herself marking numbers off the bingo card and crossing out numbers on the map that weren't represented on the card.

Henry had confiscated the letter that was contained in the envelope to see if he could read anything more into the words.

Larry,
I shouldn't be surprised that it's taking so long.
Yet, I can't comprehend how you haven't figured it out.
I don't want to do it but you're leaving me no choice.
I know where your wife and daughter are.
You have two hours if you want to see them again.
Two hours if you want to solve this case.
Don't let these women down, Larry.

Don't let the children suffer.

Henry leaned into Gemini and held the note so they could both see it. "I think the infants may be okay. This note proves that the stalker and the kidnapper are one in the same. It's not about the babies, it's about Rock. Whoever this is, they want him to suffer."

Just as Gemini opened her mouth to respond Dixie called out, "I've got it." Everyone in the station raced to the white board to see what she figured out. "We didn't need all the numbers that were given. Looking at the card compared to the placement of the numbers on the board, the only one that doesn't make sense is I eighteen. That number is our free space. If we look at the line here, our next number that would give us a bingo is O seventy-two. Every building along the diagonal is a shop of some sort until you get down here." She traced the line on the board with her fingertip until it landed directly on a church with a large cemetery in the back. "We need to get to the church."

Rock all but ran to the car and Dixie and Stone sprinted to keep up with him. Stone leaned into the passenger seat and assured Rock that his wife was safe. Three officers were now inside her room and patrol was outside the hotel covering every entrance. Rock nodded but said nothing.

She called and asked him to meet her knowing he wouldn't ever say no. "Meet me inside. Wait for me. I won't be long."

Dixie and Rock entered the church. It was smaller than it appeared from the outside. There was a narrow beam of light filtering in through the windows showing a sprinkling of dust particles floating through the air. One man sat in the first pew with his back to them. They both made their way up the center aisle and he turned to face them.

"Detectives. I should have known you'd show up."

"Travis? What are you doing here?" Rock's voice hung in the air.

"Waiting for the person you're looking for. My sister."

"Where is she?"

"My guess? Saying her goodbyes to Hope and waiting for you." He made no move to run and his voice was soft and calm, almost eerie. His eyes were empty as if this was the moment he would be free. No worried, no regrets.

"Where are the children? Are they alive?"

"The children are fine. They're at my house. I know you snooped around when you came to question me, As soon as I know my sister is safe, I'll give you the code. The locks on the closet door are simple but the door inside that leads to the basement isn't quite as easy." He tilted his head to the side and frowned. "You can wipe that look of concern off your face, they've been well taken care of. Fed, bathed, clothed. There was never any intention of harming them. The whole idea was to harm you, to take from you what you took from my sister. Then, at the last minute, Shaina backed out."

"Why me?"

He let out a gasp of air. "You really don't know? She'll have to fill you in on the details but I can tell you, she only ever wanted your attention. She believed you were soul mates. Coming from the same city, yet meeting hundreds of miles away on a last minute vacation. She tried to contact you a few months later but you acted like you had no idea who she was. She could have handled that, she would have been just fine. What she couldn't handle was, later, when she reached out to you specifically, when her daughter was kidnapped right out of her backyard, and you acted like you didn't care at all. That broke her. She knew in her heart you were the only one who could help find her daughter and you failed her, refused to take her case."

Rock stood, staring at him. He couldn't believe what he was hearing.

Travis's eyes settled on the floor and he took a deep breath. "It took them four days to find her. She was in an alleyway, wrapped in the same scarf Shaina had her in when she brought her home from the hospital. Her fragile body was mixed in with plastic bags and empty food containers. She was only four months old."

"So, I met her on vacation. That doesn't answer why I would be able to help her."

"You know. She's watched you for years. She forgave your infidelities toward her, convinced you weren't ready to settle down. And then, when your wife came around, she was upset that you took the next step and made your relationship more permanent but...she thought it was a phase. Until Emma came along. She met your wife in the hospital. She saw how you looked at Emma, how you melted around her every time you held her in your arms. Emma wasn't a phase. You couldn't just walk away. So, Shaina had to take control. She had to remind you who she was so you two could be happy together. And now? Now you've left her with nothing. She's merely pieces of the woman she used to be. And it's all your fault, detective. Because you chose, selfishly, to not give her any more of your time. You should probably give her some of it now. She's already told you where she is."

Dixie nodded toward the two officers that had remained just inside the entrance to give them the go ahead to arrest Travis. As they exited the church she showed Rock her phone. "I know where she is. I pulled up a map of the cemetery while you were talking to him. The gravestones are marked by rows and columns. O-72, our last bingo number, is down this way."

She knelt in front of the gravestone and dusted the top to remove the fine layer of dirt that had settled since her last visit. Using the edge of her sweatshirt sleeve, she traced each intricately engraved letter, slowly pronouncing her name as she did so. The hair on her arms stood upright and she shivered as a breeze pushed its way past her. She traced the numbers, recalling how she felt each day. 3/9/06. She had never known so much love for a single person, never knew one was capable of being so happy and so vulnerable at once. 7/5/06. She hadn't experienced such heartbreak ever in her life. Someone she had known less than four months had shattered her world, taking her heart, stealing her joy, her strength. Everything she had ever known was ripped away.

She turned and sat down. Once again she felt the coldness of the gravestone burrowing beneath the skin on her cheek, the book of rhymes clutched tightly in her arms. Opening the cover, her chest constricted until she could barely take a breath. "I'm going away for a while. But I want you to know I love you, with every bit of my heart. No matter where I am, I'll always be thinking of you." She flipped to the first page and choked out the words of her daughter's favorite rhyme. "The three little kittens, they lost their mittens, and they began to cry. Oh, mother dear, we sadly fear..."

They stood silently and watched her. The shattered remains of a woman who once had it all, now using what was left to make her daughter comfortable. She cleared the debris from the gravestone and they watched as she wiped the engraving clean before wrapping one of her scarves around the bottom of the stone. "Should we interrupt her or let her finish?"

"Let's give her another minute. She knows it's her last chance to be with her baby." They cautiously inched forward, listening to her recite the rhyme.

When she was done, she shifted her eyes to look up at them and pulled her head away from the gravestone.

Rock gasped when he finally saw her face. He recognized her instantly, remembered the look on her face as she sat in the hotel chair, reading this same book all those years ago. Time had not been good to her.

Shaina squinted and a disheartened smile passed across her face. "Hi, Larry. Allow me to introduce you to your daughter."

Author's Note

When you are finished reading, if you do not keep physical books, please consider donating your copy to your local library for their book sale or to your local prison book program.